LONDON'S MOST DESIRABLE DOCS

Heroes, heartbreakers…and husbands?

Amongst the glittering lights of London the hard-working doctors and nurses at The Royal are the talk of the town—and none more so than Hugh and Anton!

Passionate and dedicated, these brilliant docs spend all day saving lives and all night breaking hearts. Their own hearts are kept under lock and key…until two sexy single ladies turn their lives upside-down and force them to question everything they ever believed in!

Don't miss the
London's Most Desirable Docs duet
by Carol Marinelli

PLAYING THE PLAYBOY'S SWEETHEART

and

UNWRAPPING HER ITALIAN DOC

Both titles are available now!

Dear Reader

I have especially enjoyed writing these two stories, because the first is set in summer and it's rather lovely to watch as Emily's little holiday break becomes rather more complicated—thanks to the very charming, very blond Hugh.

Then I got to take myself straight into winter and a lovely English Christmas, with Louise determined to enjoy it this year. She's rather cheeky, *very* flirty, and absolutely the last thing that brooding, incredibly sexy Anton needs right now.

Ho, ho, ho!

And in the midst of all that along came Alex and Jennifer, tap-dancing across the stage as I tried to write—more about them later!

I love my job!

Happy reading

Carol x

UNWRAPPING HER ITALIAN DOC

BY
CAROL MARINELLI

First published in Great Britain 2014
by Mills & Boon, an imprint of Harlequin (UK) Limited,
Large Print edition 2015
Eton House, 18-24 Paradise Road,
Richmond, Surrey, TW9 1SR

© 2014 Carol Marinelli

ISBN: 978-0-263-25475-4

Harlequin (UK) Limited's policy is to use papers that are natural, renewable and recyclable products and made from wood grown in sustainable forests. The logging and manufacturing processes conform to the legal environmental regulations of the country of origin.

Printed and bound in Great Britain
by CPI Antony Rowe, Chippenham, Wiltshire

Carol Marinelli recently filled in a form where she was asked for her job title and was thrilled, after all these years, to be able to put down her answer as 'writer'. Then it asked what Carol did for relaxation. After chewing her pen for a moment Carol put down the truth—'writing'. The third question asked: 'What are your hobbies?' Well, not wanting to look obsessed or, worse still, boring, she crossed the fingers on her free hand and answered 'swimming and tennis'. But, given that the chlorine in the pool does terrible things to her highlights, and the closest she's got to a tennis racket in the last couple of years is watching the Australian Open, I'm sure you can guess the real answer!

Recent titles by Carol Marinelli:

These books are also available in eBook format from www.millsandboon.co.uk

CHAPTER ONE

'ANTON, WOULD YOU do me a favour?'

Anton Rossi's long, brisk stride was broken by the sound of Louise's voice.

He had tried very hard not to notice her as he had stepped into the maternity unit of The Royal in London, though, of course, he had.

Louise was up a stepladder and putting up Christmas decorations. Her skinny frame was more apparent this morning as she was dressed in very loose, navy scrubs with a long-sleeved, pale pink top worn underneath. Her blonde hair was tied in a high ponytail and she had layer after layer of tinsel around her neck.

She was also, Anton noted, by far too pale.

Yes, whether he had wanted to or not, he had noticed her.

He tended to notice Louise Carter a lot.

'What is it that you want?' Anton asked, as he reluctantly turned around.

'In that box, over there…' Louise raised a slender arm and pointed it towards the nurses' station '…there's some gold tinsel.'

He just stood there and Louise wondered if possibly he didn't understand what she was asking for.

'Tin-sel…' she said slowly, in the strange attempt at an Italian accent that Louise did now and then when she was trying to explain a word to him. Anton watched in concealed amusement as she jiggled the pieces around her neck. 'Tinsel, go-o-old.'

'And?'

Louise gave up on her accent. 'Could you just get it for me? I've run out of gold.'

'I'm here to check on Hannah Evans.'

'It will only take you a second,' Louise pointed out. 'Look, if I get down now I'll have to start again.' Her hand was holding one piece of gaudy green tinsel to the tired maternity wall. 'I'm trying to make a pattern.'

'You are *trying*, full stop,' Anton said, and walked off.

'Bah, humbug,' Louise called to his departing shoulders.

Anton, had moved to London from Milan and, having never spent a Christmas in England, would have to find out later what that translated as but he certainly got the gist.

Yes, he wasn't exactly in the festive spirit. For the last few years Anton had, in fact, dreaded Christmas.

Unfortunately there was no escaping it at The Royal—December had today hit and there were invites galore for Christmas lunches, dinners and parties piling into his inbox that he really ought to attend. Walking into work this morning, he had seen a huge Christmas tree being erected in the hospital foyer and now Louise had got in on the act. She seemed to be attempting to singlehandedly turn the maternity ward into Santa's grotto.

Reluctantly, *very* reluctantly, he headed over to the box, retrieved a long piece of gold tinsel and returned to Louise, who gave him a sweet smile as she took it.

Actually, no, Anton decided, it was far from a sweet smile—it was a slightly sarcastic, rather triumphant smile.

'Thank you very much,' Louise said.

'You're more than welcome,' Anton responded, and walked off.

Anton knew, just knew that if he turned around it would be to the sight of Louise poking her tongue out at him.

Keep going, he told himself.

Do not turn around, for it would just serve to encourage her and he was doing everything in his power to discourage Louise. She was the most skilled flirt he had ever come across. At first he has assumed Louise was like that with everyone—it had come as a disconcerting, if somewhat pleasant surprise to realise that the blatant flirting seemed to be saved solely for him.

Little known to Louise, he enjoyed their encounters, not that he would ever let on.

Ignore her, Anton told himself.

Yet he could not.

Anton turned to the sight of Louise on the stepladder, tongue out, fingers up and well and truly caught!

Louise actually froze for a second, which was very unfortunate, given the gesture she was making, but then she unfroze as Anton turned and walked back towards her. A shriek of nervous laughter started to pour from Louise because, from the way that Anton was walking, it felt as if he might be about to haul her from the ladder and over his shoulder. Wouldn't that be nice? both simultaneously thought, but instead he came right up to her, his face level with her groin, and looked up into china-blue eyes as she looked down at the sexiest, most aloof, impossibly arrogant man to have ever graced The Royal.

'I got you your tinsel.' Anton pointed at her and his voice was stern but, Louise noted, that sulky mouth of his was doing its level best not to smile.

'Yes, Anton, you did,' Louise said, wondering

if he could feel the blast of heat coming from her loins. God knew, he was miserable and moody but her body responded to him as if someone had just thrown another log on the fire whenever he was around.

On many levels he annoyed her—Anton checked and re-checked everything that she did, as if she was someone who had just wandered in from the street and offered to help out for the day, rather than a qualified midwife. Yet, aside from their professional differences, he was as sexy as hell and the sparks just flew off the two of them, no matter how Anton might deny that they did.

'So why this?' Anton asked, and pulled a face and poked his tongue out at her, and Louise smiled at the sight of his tongue and screwed-up features as he mimicked her gestures. He was still gorgeous—olive-skinned, his black hair was glossy and straight and so well cut that Louise constantly had to resist running her hands through it just to see it messed up. His eyes were a very dark blue and she ached to see them smile, yet, possibly for the first time, while aimed at her, now they were.

Oh, his expression was cross but, Louise could just see, those eyes were finally smiling and so she took the opportunity to let him know a few home truths.

'It's the way that you do things, Anton.' Louise attempted to explain. 'Why couldn't you just say, "Sure, Louise," and go and get the tinsel?'

'Because, as I've told you, I am on my way to see a patient.'

'Okay, why didn't you smile when you walked into the unit and saw the decorations that I've spent the last two hours putting up and say, "Ooh, that looks nice"?'

'Truth?' Anton said.

'Truth.' Louise nodded.

'I happen to think that you have too many decorations…' He watched her eyes narrow at his criticism. 'You asked why I didn't tell you how nice they looked.'

'I did,' Louise responded. 'Okay, then, third

question, why didn't you say hello to me when you walked past?'

For Anton, that was the trickiest to answer. 'Because I didn't see you.'

'Please!' Louise rolled her eyes. 'You saw me—you just chose to ignore me, as I'm going to choose to ignore your slight about my decorations. You can never have too much tinsel.'

'Oh, believe me Louise, you can,' Anton said, looking around. The corridor was a riot of red, gold and green tinsel stars. He looked up to where silver foil balloons hung from the ceilings. Then he looked down to plastic snowmen dancing along the bottom of the walls. Half of the windows to the patients' rooms had been sprayed with fake snow. Louise had clearly been busy. 'Nothing matches.' Anton couldn't help but smile and he *really* tried to help but smile! 'You don't have a theme.'

'The theme is Christmas, Anton,' Louise said in response. 'I had a very tinsel-starved Christmas last year and I intend to make up for it this one. I'm doing the nativity scene this afternoon.'

'Good for you,' Anton said, and walked off.

Louise didn't poke out her tongue again and even if she had Anton wouldn't have seen it because this time he very deliberately didn't turn around.

He didn't want to engage in conversation with Louise. He didn't want to find out why she'd had a tinsel-starved Christmas the previous year.

Or rather he *did* want to find out.

Louise was flaky, funny, sexy and everything Anton did not need to distract him at work. He wasn't here to make friends—his social life was conducted well away from the hospital walls. Anton did his level best to keep his distance from everyone at work except his patients.

'Hannah.' He smiled as he stepped into the four-bedded ward but Hannah didn't smile back and Anton pulled the curtains around her bed before asking his patient any questions. 'Are you okay?' Anton checked.

'I'm so worried.'

'Tell me,' Anton offered.

'I'm probably being stupid, I know, but Brenda

came in this morning and I said the baby had moved and I'm sure that it did, but it hasn't since then.'

'So you're lying here, imagining the worst?'

'Yes,' Hannah admitted. 'It's taken so long to get here that I'm scared something's going to go wrong now.'

'I know how hard your journey has been,' Anton said. Hannah had conceived by IVF and near the end of a tricky pregnancy she had been brought in for bed rest as her blood pressure was high and the baby's amniotic fluid was a little on the low side. Anton specialised in high-risk pregnancies and so he was very comfortable listening to Hannah's concerns.

'Let me have a feel,' Anton said. 'It is probably asleep.'

For all he was miserable with the staff and kept himself to himself, Anton was completely lovely and open with his patients. He had a feel of Hannah's stomach and then took out a Doppler machine and had a listen, locating the heartbeat straight away. 'Beautiful,' Anton said, and they listened for a moment. 'Have you had break-fast?' Anton asked, because if Hannah had low blood sugar, that could slow movements down.

'I have.'

'How many movements are you getting?'

'I felt one now,' Hanna said.

'That's because I just nudged your baby awake when I was feeling your stomach.'

He sat going through her charts. Hannah's blood pressure was at the higher limits of nor-mal and Anton wondered for a long moment how best to proceed. While the uterus was usu-ally the best incubator, there were times when the baby was safest out. He had more than a vested interested in this pregnancy and he told Hannah that. 'Do you know you will be the first patient that I have ever helped both to conceive through IVF *and* deliver their baby?'

'No.' Hannah frowned. 'I thought in your line of work that that would happen to you all the time.'

'No.' Anton shook his head. 'Remember how upset you were when I first saw you because the doctor you had been expecting was sick on the day of your egg retrieval?'

Hannah nodded and actually blushed. 'I was very rude to you.'

'Because you didn't want a locum to be taking over your care.' Anton smiled. 'And that is fair enough. In Italy I used to do obstetrics but then I moved into reproductive endocrinology and specialised there. In my opinion you can't do both simultaneously, they are completely different specialties—you have to always be available for either. I only helped out that week because Richard was sick. I still cover very occasionally to help out and also because I like to keep up to date but in truth I cannot do both.'

'So how come you moved back to obstetrics?'

'I missed it,' Anton admitted. 'I do like the fertility side of things and I do see patients where that is their issue but if they need IVF then I refer them. Obstetrics is where I prefer to be.'

The movements were slowing down. Anton could see that and with her low level of amniotic fluid, Hannah would be more aware than most of any movement. 'I think your baby might be just about cooked,' Anton said, and then headed out of the ward and asked Brenda to come in. 'I'm just going to examine Hannah,' Anton said, and spoke to both women as he did so. 'Your cervix is thinning and you're already three centimetres dilated.' He looked at Brenda. 'Kicks are down from yesterday.'

Anton had considered delivering Hannah last night and now, with the news that the kicks were down combined with Hannah's distress, he decided to go ahead this morning.

'I think we'll get things started,' Anton said.

'Now?'

'Yes.' Anton nodded and he explained to Hannah his reasoning. 'We've discussed how your placenta is coming to the end of its use-by date. Sometimes the baby does better on the outside than in and I think we've just reached that time.' He let it sink in for a moment. 'I'll start a drip, though we'll just give you a low dose to help move things along.'

Hannah called her husband and Anton spoke

with Brenda at the nurses' station, then Hannah was taken around to the delivery ward.

All births were special and precious but Anton had been concerned about Hannah for a couple of weeks as the baby was a little on the small side. Anton would actually be very relieved once this baby was out.

By the time he had set up the drip and Hannah was attached to the baby monitor, with Luke, her husband, by her side, Anton was ready for a coffee break. He checked on another lady who would soon deliver and then he checked on his other patients on the ward.

Stephanie, another obstetrician, had been on last night and had handed over to him but, though Anton respected Stephanie, he had learnt never to rely on handovers. Anton liked to see for himself where his patients were and though he knew it infuriated some of the staff it was the way he now worked and he wasn't about to change that.

Satisfied that all was well, he was just about to take himself to the staffroom when he saw Louise, still up that ladder, but she offered no snarky comment this time, neither were there any requests for assistance. Instead, she was pressing her fingers into her eyes and clearly felt dizzy.

Not my problem, Anton decided.

But, of course, it was.

CHAPTER TWO

'LOUISE…' HE WALKED over and saw her already pale features were now white, right down to her lips. 'Louise, you need to get down from the ladder.'

The sound of his voice created a small chasm between the stars dancing in her eyes and Louise opened her eyes to the sight of Anton walking towards her. And she would get down if only she could remember how her legs worked.

'Come on,' Anton said. This time he *did* take her down from the ladder, though not over his shoulder, as they had both briefly considered before. Instead, he held his hand out and she took it and shakily stepped down. Anton put a hand around her waist and led her to the staffroom, where he sat her down and then went to the fridge and got out some orange juice.

'Here,' he said, handing the glass to her.

Louise took a grateful gulp and then another and blew out a breath. 'I'm so sorry about that. I just got a bit dizzy.'

'Did you have breakfast this morning?'

'I did.' Louise nodded but he gave her a look that said he didn't believe a word. Anton then huffed off, leaving her sitting in the staffroom while he went to the kitchen. Louise could hear him feeding bread into the toaster.

God, Louise thought, rolling her eyes, here comes the lecture.

Anton returned a moment later with two slices of toast smothered in butter and honey.

'I just told you that I'd already had breakfast,' Louise said.

'I think you should eat this.'

'If I eat that I'll be sick. I just need to lie down for a few minutes.'

'Do you have a photo shoot coming up?' Anton asked, and Louise sighed. 'Answer me,' Anton said.

'Yes, I have a big photo shoot taking place

on Christmas Eve but that has no part in my nearly fainting.'

Louise was a part-time lingerie model. She completely loved her side job and took it seriously. Everyone thought that it was hilarious, everyone, that was, except Anton. Mind, he didn't find anything very funny these days.

'You're too thin.' Anton was blunt and though Louise knew it was out of concern, there was no reason for him to be. She knew only too well the reason for the little episode on the ladder.

'Actually, I'm not too thin, I'm in the healthy weight range,' Louise said. 'Look, I just got dizzy. Please don't peg me as having an eating disorder just because I model part time.'

'My sister is a model in Milan,' Anton said, and Louise could possibly have guessed that, had Anton had a sister, then a model she might be because Anton really was seriously beautiful.

Louise lay down on the sofa because she could still see stars and she didn't want Anton to know that. In fact, she just wanted him gone. And she knew how to get rid of him! A little flirt would have him running off.

'Are my hips not childbearing enough for you, Anton?' Louise teased, and Anton glanced down and it wasn't a baby he was thinking about between those legs!

No way!

Louise had used to work in Theatre—in fact, she had been the nurse who had scrubbed in on his first emergency Caesarean here at The Royal. It had been the first emergency Caesarean section he had performed since losing Alberto. Of course, Louise hadn't known just how nervous Anton had been that day and she could not possibly have guessed how her presence had both helped and unsettled him.

During surgery Anton had been grateful for a very efficient scrub nurse and one who had immediately worked well with him.

After surgery, when he'd gone to check in on the infant, Louise had been there, smiling and cooing at the baby. She had turned around and congratulated him on getting the baby out in time, and he had actually forgotten to thank her for her help in Theatre.

Possibly he had snapped an order instead— anything rather than like her.

Except he did.

A few months ago Louise had decided to more fully utilise her midwifery training and had come to work on Maternity, which was, of course, Anton's stomping ground.

Seeing her most days, resisting her on each and every one of them, was quietly driving him insane.

She was very direct, a bit off the wall and terribly beautiful too, and if she hadn't worked here Anton would not hesitate.

Mind you, if she hadn't worked here he wouldn't know just how clever and funny she was.

Anton looked down where she lay, eyes closed on the sofa, and saw there was a touch of colour coming back to her cheeks and her breathing was nice and regular now. Then Anton pulled his eyes up from the rise and fall of her chest and instead of leaving the room he met her very blue eyes.

Louise could see the concern was still there. 'Honestly, Anton, I didn't get dizzy because I have an eating disorder,' Louise said, and, because this was the maternity ward and such things were easily discussed, especially if your name was Louise, she told him what the real problem was. 'I've got the worst period in the history of the world, if you must know.'

'Okay.' He looked at her very pale face and her hand that moved low onto her stomach and decided she was telling the truth.

'Do you need some painkillers?'

'I've had some,' Louise said, closing her eyes. 'They didn't do a thing.'

'Do you need to go home?' Anton asked.

'Are you going to write me a note, Doctor?'

He watched her lips turn up in a smile as she teased but then shook her head. 'No, I'll be fine soon, though I might just stay lying down here for a few minutes.'

'Do you want me to let Brenda know?'

'Please.' Louise nodded.

'You're sure I can't get you anything?' Anton checked.

'A heat pack would be lovely,' Louise said, glad that her eyes were closed because she could imagine his expression at being asked to fetch a heat pack, when surely that was a nurse's job. 'It needs two minutes in the microwave,' she called, as he walked out.

It took five minutes for Anton to locate the heat packs and so he returned seven minutes later to where she lay, knees up with her eyes closed, and he placed the heat pack gently over her uterus.

'You make a lovely midwife,' Louise said, feeling the weight and the warmth.

'I've told Brenda,' Anton said, 'and she said that you are to take your time and come back when you're ready.' He went to go but she still concerned him and Anton walked over and sat down by her waist on the sofa where she lay.

Louise felt him sit down beside her and then he picked up her hand. She knew that he was checking her nails for signs of anaemia and she was about to make a little tease about her not knowing he cared, except Anton this close made talking impossible. She opened her eyes and he pulled down her lower lids and she wished, oh, how she wished, those fingers were on her face for very different reasons.

'You're anaemic,' Anton said.

'I'm on iron and folic acid...'

'You're seeing someone?'

'Yes, but I...' Louise had started to let a few close friends know what was going on in her personal life but she wasn't quite ready to tell the world just yet. She ached to discuss it with Anton, not on a personal level but a professional one, yet was a little shy to. 'I've spoken to my GP.' His pager went off and though he read it he still sat there, but the moment had gone and Louise decided not to tell him her plans and what was going on.

'He's told you that you don't have to struggle like this. There is the Pill and there is also an IUD that can give you a break from menstr—'

'Anton,' Louise interrupted. 'My GP is a she, and I *am* a midwife, which means, oh, about ten times a day I give contraceptive advice, so I do know these things.'

'Then you should know that you don't have to put up with this.'

'I do. Thanks for your help,' Louise said, and then, aware of her snappy tone, she halted. After all, he was just trying to help. He simply didn't know what was going on in her world. 'I owe you one.' She gave him a smile. 'I'll buy you a drink tonight.'

'Tonight?' Anton frowned.

'It's the theatre Christmas do,' Louise said, and Anton inwardly groaned, because another non-work version of Louise seared into his brain he truly did not need! Anton had seen Louise dressed to the nines a few times since he had started here and it was a very appealing sight. He had braced himself for the maternity do in a couple of weeks—in fact, he had a date lined up for that night—but it had never entered his head that Louise would be at the theatre do tonight.

'So you will be going tonight?' Anton checked. 'Even though you're not feeling well?'

'Of course I'm going,' Louise said. 'I worked there for five years.' She opened her eyes and gave him a very nice smile, though their interlude was over. Concerned Anton had gone and he was back to bah, humbug as he stood. 'I'll see you tonight, Anton.'

Stop the drip! Anton wanted to say as he went in to check on Hannah, for he would dearly love a reason to be stuck at the hospital tonight.

Of course, he didn't stop the drip and instead Hannah progressed beautifully.

'Louise, would you be able to go and work in Delivery after lunch?' Brenda came over as Louise added the finishing touches to her nativity scene during her lunch break. She'd taken her chicken and avocado salad out with her and was eating it as she arranged all the pieces. 'Angie called in sick and we're trying to get an agency nurse.'

Louise had to stop herself from rolling her

eyes. While she loved being in Delivery for an entire shift, she loathed being sent in for a couple of hours. Louise liked to be there for her patient for the entire shift.

'Sure,' Louise said instead.

'They're a bit short now,' Brenda pushed, and Louise decided not to point out that she'd only had fifteen minutes' break, given the half-hour she'd taken earlier that morning. So, instead, she popped the cutest Baby Jesus ever into the crib, covered him in a little rug and headed off to Delivery.

She took the handover, read through Hannah's birth plan then went in and said hello to Hannah and Luke. Hannah had been a patient on the ward for a couple of weeks now so introductions had long since been done.

Hannah was lying on her side and clearly felt uncomfortable.

'It really hurts.'

'I know that it does,' Louise said, showing Luke a nice spot to rub on the bottom of

Hannah's back, but Hannah kept pushing his hand away.

'Do you want to have a little walk?' Louise offered, and at first Hannah shook her head but then agreed. Louise sorted out the drip and got her up off the delivery bed and they shuffled up and down the corridor, sometimes silent between contractions, when Hannah leant against the wall, other times talking.

'I still can't believe we'll have a baby for Christmas,' Hannah said.

'How exciting.' Louise smiled. 'Have you shopped for the baby?''

'Not yet!' Hannah shook her head. 'Didn't want the bad luck.' She leant against the wall and gave a very low moan and then another one.

'Let's get you back,' Louise said, guiding the drip as Luke helped his wife.

Hannah didn't like the idea of sitting on a birthing ball—in fact, she climbed back onto the delivery bed and went back to lying on her side as Louise checked the baby's heart, which was fine.

'You're doing wonderfully, Hannah,' Louise said.

'I can't believe we're going to get our baby,' Hannah said. 'We tried for ages.'

'I know that you did,' Louise said.

'I'm so lucky to have Anton,' Hannah said. 'He got me pregnant!'

Louise looked over at Luke and they shared a smile because at this stage of labour women said the strangest things at times, only Louise's smile turned into a slight frown as Luke explained what she'd meant. 'Anton was the one who put back the embryo…'

'Oh!' Louise said, more than a little surprised, because that was something she hadn't known—yes, of course he would deal with infertility to a point, but it was a very specific specialty and for Anton to have performed the embryo transfer confused Louise.

'He was a reproductive specialist in Milan, one of the top ones,' Luke explained further, when he saw Louise's frown. 'We thought we were getting a fill-in doctor when Richard, the specialist overseeing Hannah's treatment, got sick, but it turned out we were getting one of the best.' He looked up as Anton came in. 'I was just telling Louise that you were the one who got Hannah pregnant.'

Anton gave a small smile of acknowledgement of the conversation then he turned to Louise. 'How is she?'

'Very well.'

Anton gave another brief nod and went to examine Hannah.

Hannah was doing very well because things soon started to get busy and by four o'clock, just when Louise should be heading home to get ready for tonight, she was cheering Hannah on.

'Are you okay, Louise?' Brenda popped her head in to see if Louise wanted one of the late staff to come in and take over but instead Louise smiled and nodded. 'I'm fine, Brenda,' Louise said. 'We're nearly there.'

She would never leave so close to the end of

a birth, Anton knew that, and she was enthusiastic at every birth, even if the mother was in Theatre, unconscious.

'How much longer?' Hannah begged.

'Not long,' Louise said. 'Don't push, just hold it now.' Louise was holding Hannah's leg and watched as the head came out and Anton carefully looped a rather thin and straggly umbilical cord from around the baby's neck.

She and Anton actually worked well in this part. Anton liked how Louise got into it and encouraged the woman no end, urging her on when required, helping him to slow things down too, if that was the course of action needed. This was the case here, because the baby was only thirty-five weeks and also rather small for dates.

'Oh, Hannah!' Louise was ecstatic as the shoulders were delivered and Anton placed the slippery bundle on Hannah's stomach and Louise rubbed the baby's back. They all watched as he took his first breath and finally Hannah and Luke had their wish come true.

'He's beautiful,' Hannah said, examining her

son in awe, holding his tiny hand, scarcely able
to believe she had a son.

He was small, even for thirty-five weeks, and,
having delivered the placenta, Anton could well
see why. The baby had certainly been delivered
at the right time and could now get the nourish-
ment he needed from his mother to fatten up.

Anton came and looked at the baby. The paediatrician was finishing up checking him over
as Louise watched.

'He looks good,' Anton said.

'So good,' Louise agreed, and then smiled at
the baby's worried-looking face. He was wearing the concerned expression that a lot of small-
for-dates babies had. 'And so hungry!'

The paediatrician went to have a word with
the parents to explain their baby's care as Louise wrapped him up in a tight parcel and popped
a little hat on him.

'How does it feel,' Louise asked Anton, 'to
have been there at conception and delivery?'
She started to laugh at her own question. 'That
sounds rude! You know what I mean.'

'I was just saying to Hannah this morning that it has never happened to me before. So this little one is a bit more special,' Anton admitted. 'I'm going to go and write my notes. I'll be back to check on Hannah in a while.'

'Well, I'll be going home soon,' Louise said, 'but I'll pass it all on.' She picked up the baby. 'Come on, little man, let's get you back to your mum.'

She didn't rush home then either, though. Louise helped with the baby's first feed, though he quickly tired and would need gavage top-ups. Having put him under a warmer beside his parents, she then went and made Hannah a massive mug of tea. Anton, who was getting a cup of tea of his own, watched as she went into her pocket and took out a teabag.

'Why do you keep teabags in your pocket?'

'Would you want that…' she sneered at the hospital teabags on the bench '…if you'd just pushed a baby out?'

'No.'

'There's your answer, then. I make sure my

mums get one nice cup of tea after they've given birth and then they wonder their entire stay in hospital why the rest of them taste so terrible after that,' Louise said. 'It's my service to women.' She went back into her pocket and gave him a teabag and Anton took it because the hospital tea really was that bad. 'Here, but that's *not* the drink I owe you for this morning. You'll get that later.'

He actually smiled at someone who wasn't a patient. 'I'll see you tonight,' Louise said, and their eyes met, just for a second but Anton was the one who looked away, and with good reason.

Yes, Anton thought, she would see him tonight but here endeth the flirting.

CHAPTER THREE

LOUISE LIVED FAIRLY close to the hospital and arrived at her small terraced home just after five to a ringing phone.

She did consider not answering it because she was already running late but, seeing that it was her mum, Louise picked up.

'I can't talk for long,' Louise warned, and then spent half an hour chatting about plans for Christmas Day.

'Mum!' Louise said, for the twentieth time. 'I'm on days off after Christmas Eve all the way till after New Year. I've told you that I'll be there for Christmas Day.'

'You said you'd be there last year,' Susan pointed out.

'Can we not go through that again,' Louise said, regretting the hurt she had caused last year by not telling her parents the truth about what had been going on in her life. 'I was just try-ing to—'

'Well, don't ever do that again,' Susan said. 'I can't bear that you chose to spend Christmas miserable and alone in some hotel rather than coming home to your family.'

'You know why I did, Mum,' Louise said, and then conceded, 'But I know now that I should have just come home.' She flicked the lights of her Christmas tree to on, smiling as she did so. 'Mum, I honestly can't wait for Christmas.'

'Neither can I. I've ordered the turkey,' Susan said, 'and I'm going to try something extra-spe-cial for Boxing Day—kedgeree…'

'Is that the thing with fish and eggs?' Louise checked.

'And curry powder,' Susan agreed.

'That's great, Mum,' Louise said, pulling a face because her mother was the worst cook in the world. The trouble was, though, that Susan considered herself an amazing cook! Louise ached for her dad sometimes, he was the kindest, most patient man, only that had proved part of the problem—the compliments he'd first given had gone straight to Susan's head and, in the kitchen, she thought she could do no wrong.

'Mum, I'd love to chat more but I have to go now and get ready, it's the theatre Christmas night out. I'll call you soon.'

'Well, enjoy.'

'I shall.'

'Oh, one other thing before you go,' Susan said. 'Did you get the referral for the specialist?'

'Not yet,' Louise sighed. 'She says she wants me to have a full six months off the Pill before she refers me…' Louise thought for a moment. She really wasn't happy with her GP. 'I know I said that I didn't want to go to The Royal for this but it might be the best place.'

'I think you're right,' Susan said. 'I didn't like to say so at the time but I don't think she took you very seriously.'

Louise nodded then glanced at the clock. So much for a quick chat!

'I have to get ready, Mum.'

'Well, if you do go to The Royal, let me know when and I'll come with you...'

'I will,' Louise said, and then there were all the *I love you*s and *Do you want a quick word with Dad?*

Louise smiled as she put down the phone because, apart from her cooking, Louise knew that she had the best mum and possibly the best family in the world.

Her dad was the most patient person and Louise's two younger sisters were amazing young women who rang Louise often, and they all got on very well.

This was part of the reason why she hadn't wanted to spoil Christmas for everyone last year and had pretended that something had happened at work. At the time it had seemed kinder to say that they were short-staffed rather than arrive home in such a fragile state on Christmas morning and ruin everyone's day.

Her sisters looked up to her and often asked her opinion on guys; it had been hard, admitting how badly she had judged Wesley. Even a part of the truth had hurt them and her dad would just about die if he knew even half of what had really gone on.

Louise lay on her bed while her bath was running, thinking back to that terrible time. Not just the break-up with Wesley but the horrible lonely time before it.

Louise's wings had been clipped during their relationship. *Seriously* clipped, to the point that she had given up her modelling side job, which she loved. Somehow, she wasn't quite sure how it had happened, her hems had got lower, her hair darker until her sparkle had almost been extinguished.

At a work function Wesley had loathed that she had chatted with Rory, an anaesthetist who was also ex-boyfriend of Louise's from way back.

She and Rory had remained very good friends up to that point.

Louise had given Wesley the benefit of the doubt after that first toxic row. Yes, she'd decided, it wasn't unreasonable for him to be jealous that she was so friendly with her ex. She had severed things with Rory, which had been hard to do and had caused considerable hurt when she had.

It hadn't stopped there, though.

Wesley hadn't liked Emily, Louise's close friend, either. He hadn't liked their odd nights out or their phone calls and texting and gradually that had all tapered off too.

Finally, realising that she had been constantly walking on eggshells and that she'd barely recognised herself any more, Louise had known she had to end things. It had been far easier said than done, though, knowing, with Wesley's building temper, that the ending would be terrible.

It had been.

On Christmas Eve, when Wesley had decided that her family didn't like him and perhaps it should be just the two of them for Christmas, Louise had known she had to get the hell out. An argument had ensued and the gentle, happy Louise had finally lost her temper.

No, he hadn't taken it well.

It would soon be a year to the very day since it

had happened, and in the year that had followed Louise had found herself again—the woman she had been before Wesley, the happy person she had once been, though it had taken a while.

Louise's confidence had been severely shaken around men but her dad, her uncles, Rory, Emily's now-husband, Hugh, all the people Wesley had been so jealous of had been such huge support—insisting that Wesley wasn't in the regular mould men were cast from. Finally convincing her that she should simply be her sparkling, annoying, once irrepressible self.

Without her family and friends, Louise did not know how she'd have survived emotionally.

She'd never turn her back on them again.

Anton had appeared at The Royal around March and the jolt of attraction had been so intense Louise had felt her mojo dash back. Possibly because he was so aloof and just so unobtainable that it had felt safe to test her flirting wings on him.

Anton never really responded, yet he never

stopped her either. He simply let her be, which was nice.

It was all for fun, a little confidence boost as she slowly returned to her old self, yet in the ensuing months it had gathered steam.

Nope!

Louise got of the bed and looked around her room. It was a sexy boudoir indeed, thanks to a few freebies from a couple of photo shoots. There was a velvet red chair that went with the velvet bedspread, and it made Louise smile every time she sat in it. She smiled even more at the thought of Anton in here but she pushed that thought aside.

In the flirting department he was divine but his arrogance, the way he double-checked everything Louise did at work, rendered him far from relationship material.

Not that she knew if he even liked her.

To Louise, Anton was a very confusing man.

Still, flirting was fun!

Not that she felt particularly sparkly tonight.

After her bath, Louise did her make-up carefully, topped it off with loads of red lipstick and then started to dry her hair.

It still fell to the right, even after nearly a year of parting it to fall to the left.

Louise examined the shiny red scar on her scalp for a moment. She could still see the needle marks. Thanks to her delay in getting sutured, the stitches had had to stay in for ten days. Unable to deal with the memory, she quickly moved on and tonged her hair into wild ringlets. She put on the Christmas holly underwear that she'd modelled a couple of months ago, along with the stockings from the same range, which were a very sheer red with green sprigs of holly and little red dots for berries.

They were fabulous!

As were the red dress and high-heeled shoes.

Hearing Emily blast the horn outside, Louise pushed out a smile, determined to enjoy all the celebrations that took place at her very favourite time of the year, however unwell she felt.

'God help Anton!' Hugh said, as Louise

stepped out of her house and waved to him and Emily.

'Why haven't they got it on?' Emily asked, as Louise dashed back in the house to check that she'd turned off her curling tongs.

'I don't know,' Hugh mused. 'Though I thought that Louise had sworn off men.'

'She's sworn off relationships,' Emily said, 'not joined a nunnery.'

Hugh laughed. No, he could not imagine Louise in a nunnery.

'Is Anton seeing anyone?' Emily asked, but Hugh shook his head.

'I don't think so—mind you, Anton's not exactly friendly and chatty.'

'He is to me.'

'Because you're six months pregnant and his patient,' Hugh pointed out, as Louise came down her path for the second time. 'Maybe you could ask him if he's seeing someone next time you see him.'

'That's a good idea.' Emily smiled. 'I'll just

slip that question in while he examines me, shall I?'

She turned and smiled as Louise got into the back of the car.

'Hi, Emily. You make a lovely taxi driver—thank you for this,' Louise said. 'Hi, Hugh, how lucky you are to have a pregnant wife over Christmas!'

'Very lucky,' Hugh agreed, as Emily drove off.

'You look gorgeous, Louise,' Emily said.

'Thank you, but I feel like crap,' Louise happily admitted. 'I've got the worst period and I can only have one eggnog as I'm working in the morning.'

Hugh arched his neck at Louise's openness and Emily smiled.

They both loved her.

As they arrived at the rather nice venue, Louise got her first full-length look at Emily.

'You look gorgeous and I want one…' she said, referring to Emily's six–months-pregnant belly, which was tonight dressed in black and looking amazing.

'You will soon,' Emily said, because Louise had shared with her her plans to get pregnant next year.

'I hope so.'

Louise's eyes scanned the room. It had been very tastefully decorated—there were pale pinkish gold twigs in vases on the tables and pale pinkish gold decorations and lights that twinkled, and there was Anton, talking to Alex, who was Hugh's boss, and Rory was with them as well.

Perfect, Louise thought as the trio made their way over and all the hellos began.

'Aren't the decorations gorgeous?' Emily said, but Louise pulled a face.

'Some colour would be nice. Who would choose pink for Christmas decorations?' As a waiter passed with a tray, she took a mini pale pink chocolate that the waiter called a frosted snowball but even the coconut was pink. 'They have a *theme*,' she said, and smiled at Anton, but it went to the wall because he wasn't looking at her.

'No Jennifer?' Hugh checked with Alex, because normally his wife Jennifer accompanied him on nights such as this.

'No, Josie's got a fever.' Alex explained things a little better for Anton. 'Josie's our youngest child. You haven't yet met my wife Jennifer, have you?'

'Your wife?' Anton said. 'I have heard a lot of nice things.'

Perhaps because Louise was close to PhD level in Anton's facial features, Anton's accent, Anton's words, oh, just everything Anton, she frowned just a little at his slightly vague response. Still, she didn't dwell on it for long because he simply looked fantastic in an evening suit. Her eyes swept his body, taking in his long legs, his very long black leather shoes and then, when her mind darted to rude places, she looked up. His olive complexion was accentuated by the white of his shirt and he was just so austere that it made her want to jump onto his lap and whisper in his ear all the things she wanted him to do to her for Christmas.

Oh, a relationship might not be on the agenda but so pointed was his dismissal of her tonight that they were clearly both thinking sex.

'Is that holly on your stockings?' Rory asked, and everyone looked down to examine Louise's long legs.

Everyone, that was, but Anton.

'Yes, I got them free after that shoot I did a couple of months ago,' Louise said. 'I've been dying to wear them ever since. Got to get into the Christmas spirit. Speaking of which, does anyone want a drink?'

'No, thank you,' Alex said.

'I'll have a tomato juice,' Emily sighed. 'A virgin bloody Mary.'

'Hugh?' Louise asked.

'I'd love an eggnog.'

'Yay!' Louise said. 'Anton?'

'No, thank you.'

'Are you sure?' Louise said. 'I thought I owed you one.'

'I'm fine,' he responded, barely looking at her.

'I think Saffarella is getting me a drink. Here she is…'

Here she was, indeedy!

Rippling black hair, chocolate-brown eyes, a figure to die for, and she was so seriously stunning that she actually made Louise feel drab, especially when her thick Italian accent purred around every name as introductions were made.

'Em-il-ee, Loo-ease.'

On sight the two women bristled.

It was like two cats meeting in the back yard and Louise almost felt her tail bush up as they both smiled and nodded.

'Sorry, I didn't catch your name,' Louise said.

Saffarella was already getting on her nerves.

'Saffarella,' she repeated in her beautiful, treacle voice, and then was kind enough to give Louise a further explanation. 'Like Cinderella.'

With a staph infection attached, Louise thought, but thankfully Rory knew Louise's humour and decided to move her on quickly!

'I'll come and help you with the drinks.' Rory

took Louise's arm and they both walked over to the bar.

'Good God!' Louise said the second they were out of earshot.

'No wonder you've got nowhere with him.' Rory laughed. 'She's stunning.'

'Oh!' Louise was seriously rattled, she was far too used to being the best-looking woman in the room. 'What sort of name is Saffarella? Well, there goes my fun for the night. I thought I'd at least get a dance with him. I don't have anyone to fancy any more,' Louise sighed. 'And I'm going to look like a wallflower.'

'Don't worry, Louise.' Rory smiled. 'I'll dance with you.'

'You have to now,' Louise said. 'I'm not having him seeing me sitting on my own. I was so positive that he liked me.'

Louise returned with Emily's virgin bloody Mary but then she caught sight of Connor and Miriam and excused herself and headed over for a good old catch up with ex-colleagues. It was actually a good, if not brilliant night—Rory was as good as his word and midway through proceedings he did dance with her.

Rory was lovely, possibly one of the nicest men that a woman could know.

In fact, Rory was the last really nice boyfriend that Louise had had.

There was absolutely nothing going on between them. Their parting, three years ago, had been an amicable one. Though most people lied when they said that, in Rory and Louise's case it had been true. Just a few weeks into their relationship Louise had, while undergoing what she'd thought were basic investigations for her erratic menstrual cycle, received the confronting news that, when the time came, she might not fall pregnant very easily.

It hadn't been a complete bombshell, Louise had known things hadn't been right, but when it had finally dropped Louise had been inconsolable. Rory had put his hands up in the end and had said that, as much as he liked her, there wasn't enough there to be talking baby, baby, baby every day of the week.

They were far better as exes than as a couple.

'How's Christmas behaving?' Rory asked, as they danced.

'Much better this time.'

'You look so much happier.'

'I'm sorry we stopped being friends,' Louise said.

'We never stopped being friends,' Rory said. 'Well, I didn't. I was so worried when you were with him.'

'I know,' Louise said. 'Thanks for being there for me.' She gave him a smile. 'I might have some happy news soon.'

'What are you up to, Louise?'

'I'm going to be trying for a baby,' Louise admitted, 'by myself.'

'How did I not guess that?' Rory smiled.

'Please don't ask me if I've thought about it.'

'I wouldn't. I know that it's all you think about.'

'It's got worse since I've gone back to midwifery,' Louise said. 'My fallopian tubes want to reach out and steal all the little babies.'

'It might end any chance of things between you and Anton,' Rory said gently, but Louise just shrugged.

'He's the last person I'd go out with, he's way too controlling and moody for my taste. I just wanted a loan of that body for a night or two.' Louise smiled. 'Nope…' She had made up her mind. In the three years since she and Rory had broken up she had made some poor choices when it came to men. The news that she might have issues getting pregnant had seriously rocked Louise's world, leaving her a touch vulnerable and exposed. She was so much stronger now, though her desire to become a mother had not diminished an inch. 'I want a baby far more than I want another failed relationship.'

'Fair enough.'

They danced on, Louise with her mind on Anton. She was seriously annoyed at the sight of them laughing and talking as they danced and the way Saffarella ran her hands through his hair and over his bum had Louise burn with jealousy.

Worse, though, was the way Anton laughed a deep laugh at something she must have said.

'I don't think I've ever seen him laugh till now, and I know that I'm funnier than her,' Louise grumbled. 'God, why does she have to be so, so beautiful? What did he introduce her as?'

'Saffarella.'

'Did he say girlfriend when he introduced her?' Louise pushed. 'Or my wife…?' She was clutching at straws as she remembered that his sister was a model. 'It's not his sister, is it?'

'If it's his sister then we should consider calling the police!' Rory said. 'Sorry, Louise, they're on together.'

But then a little while later came the good news!

She and Rory were enjoying another dance, imagining things that could never happen to John Lennon's 'Imagine'. Louise was thinking of Anton while Rory was thinking of a woman who couldn't be here tonight. He glanced up and saw that Anton was watching them, and then Anton looked over again.

'Anton keeps looking over,' Rory whispered in Louise's ear.

'Really?'

'He does,' Rory said. 'I don't think he likes me any more—in fact, I'd say from the look I just got he wants to take me out the back and knock my lights out.'

'Seriously?' Louise was delighted at the turn of events.

'Well, not quite that much, but I think you may be be right, Louise, Anton does like you.'

'I told you that he did. Is he still looking?'

'He's trying not to.'

'You have to kiss me,' Louise said.

'No.'

'Please.' Louise was insistent. 'Just one long one—it will serve him bloody right for trying to make me jealous. Come on, Rory,' she said when, instead of kissing her, he still shook his head. 'It's not like we never have before and I do it all the time when I'm modelling. It doesn't mean anything.'

'No,' Rory said.

'I got off with you a couple of years ago when Gina got drunk and was making a play for you!' Louise reminded him.

Gina was an anaesthetist who had had a drink and drug problem and had gone into treatment a few months ago. A couple of years back Rory had been trying to avoid Gina at a Christmas party. Gina had tended to make blatant plays for him when drunk, so he and Louise had had a kiss and pretended to leave together.

'Come on, Rory.'

'No,' he said, and then he rolled his eyes and reluctantly admitted the reason why not. 'I like someone.'

'Who?' Louise's curiosity was instant.

'Just someone.'

'Is she here?'

'No,' Rory said. 'But I don't want it getting back to her that I got off with my ex.'

'Do I know her?'

'Leave it, Louise,' Rory said. 'Please.'

It really was turning out to be the most frustrating night! First Anton and Saffarella, now Rory with his secret.

Hugh and Emily watched the action from the safety of the tables, trying to work out just what was going on.

'Anton is holding Saffarella like a police riot shield,' Hugh observed, but Emily laughed just a little too late.

'Are you okay?' Hugh checked, looking at his wife, who, all of a sudden, was unusually quiet.

'I'm a bit tired,' Emily admitted.

'Do you want to go home?' Hugh checked, and Emily nodded. 'But I promised Louise a lift.'

'She'll be fine,' Hugh said, standing as Louise and Rory made their way over from the dance floor. 'We're going to go,' Hugh said. 'Emily's a bit tired.'

'Emily?' Louise frowned as she looked at her friend. 'Are you okay?'

'Can I not just be tired?' Emily snapped, and then corrected herself. 'Sorry, Louise. Look, I know that I said I'd give you a lift—'

'Don't be daft,' Louise interrupted. 'Go home to bed.'

'I'll see Louise home,' Rory said, and Hugh gave a nod of thanks.

They said their goodnights but as Hugh and Emily walked off, Rory could see the concern on Louise's face.

'Louise!' Rory knew what she was thinking and dismissed it. 'Emily's fine. It isn't any wonder that she's feeling tired. She's six months pregnant and working. Theatre was really busy today...'

'I guess, but...' Louise didn't know what to say. Rory didn't really get her intuition where pregnant women were concerned. She wasn't about to explain it to him again but he'd already guessed what she was thinking.

'Not your witch thing again?' Rory sighed.

'Midwives know.' Louise nodded. 'I'm honestly worried.'

'Come on, I'll get you a drink,' Rory said. 'You can have two eggnogs.' But Louise shook her head. 'I just want to go home,' she admitted. 'You stay, I can get a taxi.'

'Don't be daft,' Rory said, and, not thinking, he put his arm around her and they headed out, followed by the very disapproving eyes of Anton.

Rory dropped her home and, though tired, Louise couldn't sleep. She looked at the crib, still wrapped in Cellophane, that she had hidden in her room, in case Emily dropped round. It was a present Louise had bought. It was stunning and better still it had been on sale. Louise had chosen not to say anything to Emily, knowing how superstitious first-time mums were about not getting anything in advance.

Emily had already been through an appendectomy at six weeks' gestation, as well as marrying Hugh and sorting out stuff with her difficult family. She was due to finish working in the New Year and finally relax and enjoy the last few weeks of pregnancy.

Louise lay there fretting, trying to tell herself that this time she was wrong.

It was very hard to understand let alone explain it but Emily had had that *look* that Louise knew too well.

Please, no!

It really was too soon.

CHAPTER FOUR

ANTON WAS RARELY uncomfortable with women.

Even the most beautiful ones.

He and Saffarella went back a long way, in a very loose way. They had met through his sister a couple of years ago and saw each other now and then. He had known that she would be in London over Christmas and Saffarella had, in fact, been the date he had planned to take to the maternity Christmas evening.

'Where are we going?' Saffarella frowned, because she clearly thought they were going back to his apartment but instead they had turned the opposite way.

'I thought I might take you back to the hotel,' Anton said.

'And are you coming in?' Saffarella asked, and gave a slightly derisive snort at Anton's lack of response. 'I guess that means, no, you're not.'

'It's been a long day…' Anton attempted, but Saffarella knew very well the terms of their friendship and it was *this* part of the night that she had been most looking forward to and she argued her case in loud Italian.

'Don't give me that, Anton. Since when have you ever been too tired? I saw you looking at that blonde tart…'

'Hey!' Anton warned, but his instant defence of Louise, combined with the fact that they both knew just who he was referring to, confirmed that Anton's mind had been elsewhere tonight. Saffarella chose to twist the knife as they pulled into the hotel. 'I doubt that she's being dropped off home by that Rory. They couldn't even wait for the night to finish to get out of the place.' When the doorman opened the door for her Saffarella got out of the car. 'Don't you ever do that to me again.' She didn't wait for the doorman, instead slamming the door closed.

Anton copped it because he knew that he deserved it.

His intention had never been to use Saffarella,

they were actually good together. Or had been. Occasionally.

Anton had never, till now, properly considered just how attracted he really was to Louise. Oh, she was the reason he had called Saffarella and asked if she was free tonight, and Saffarella had certainly used him in the same way at times.

But it wasn't just the ache of his physical attraction to Louise that was the problem. He liked her. A lot. He liked her humour, her flirting, the way she just openly declared whatever was on her mind, not that he'd ever tell her that.

But knowing she was on with Rory, knowing he had taken her home, meant that Anton just wanted to be alone tonight to sulk.

It's your own fault, Anton, he said to himself as he drove home.

He should have asked Louise out months ago but then he reminded himself of the reason he hadn't, couldn't, wouldn't be getting involved with anyone from work ever again.

Approaching four years ago, Christmas Day had suddenly turned into a living nightmare.

Telling parents on Christmas Day that their new-born baby was going to die was hell at the best of times.

But at the worst of times, telling parents, while knowing that the death could have been avoided, was a hell which Anton could not yet escape from and he returned to the nightmare time and again.

The shouts and the accusations from Alberto's father, Anton could still hear some nights before going to sleep.

The coroner's report had pointed to a string of communication errors but found that it had been no one person's fault in particular. Anton could recite it off by heart, because he had gone over and over and over it, trying to see what he could have done differently.

But the year in the between the death and the coroner's report had been one Anton could rarely stand to recall.

He took his foot off the brake as he realised he was speeding and pulled over for a moment because he could not safely think about that time and drive.

His relationship hadn't survived either. Dahnya, his girlfriend at the time, had been one of the midwives on duty that Christmas morning and when she hadn't called him, the continual excuses she had made instead of accepting her part in the matter, had proved far too much for them.

Friends and colleagues had all been injected with the poison of gossip. Everyone had raced to cover their backs by stabbing others in theirs and the once close, supportive unit he had been a part of had turned into a war zone.

Anton had been angry too.

Furious.

He had raged when he had seen that information had not been passed on to him. Information that would have meant he would have come to see and then got the labouring mother into Theatre far sooner than he had.

The magic had gone from obstetrics and even before the coroner's findings had been in,

Anton had moved into reproductive endocrinology, immersing himself in it, honing his skills, concentrating on the maths and conundrum of infertility. It had absorbed him and he had enjoyed it, especially the good times—when a woman who had thought she never would get pregnant finally did, and yet more and more he had missed obstetrics.

To go back to it, Anton had known he would need a completely fresh start, for he no longer trusted his old colleagues. He had come to London and really had done his best to put things behind him.

It was not so easy, though, and he was aware that he tended to take over. He sat there and thought about his first emergency Caesarean at The Royal. Louise just so brisk and efficient and completely in sync with him as they'd fought to get the deteriorating baby out.

He had slept more easily that night.

That hurdle he had passed and perhaps things would have got better. Perhaps he might have started to hand over the reins to skilled hands a touch further had Gina not rear-ended him in the hospital car park.

Anton had got out, taken one look at her, parked her car, pocketed the keys and then driven her home.

Twenty minutes later he'd reported her to the chief of Anaesthetics and Anton had been hyper-vigilant ever since then.

Anton looked down the street at the Christmas lights but they offered no reprieve; instead, they made it worse. He loathed Christmas. Alberto, the baby, had missed out on far too many.

Yep, Anton reminded himself as he drove home and then walked into his apartment, which had not a single shred of tinsel or a decoration on display, there was a very good reason not to get involved with Louise or anyone at work.

He took out his work phone and called the ward to check on a couple of patients, glad to hear that all was quiet tonight.

Anton poured a drink and pulled out his other phone, read an angry text from Saffarella, telling him he should find someone else for the maternity night out, followed by a few insults that Anton knew she expected a response to.

He was too tired for a row and too disengaged for an exchange of texts that might end up in bed.

Instead, he picked up his work phone and scrolled through some texts. All the staff knew they could contact him and with texting often it was easy just to send some obs through or say you were on your way.

He scrolled through and looked at a couple of Louise's messages.

BP 140/60—and yes, Santa, before you ask, I've read your list and I've checked it twice—it's still 140/60. From your little helper

He'd had no idea what that little gem had meant until he'd been in a department store, with annoying music grating in his ears, and a song had come on and he'd burst out laughing there and then.

He had realised then how lame his response at the time had been.

Call me if it goes up again.

Her response:

Bah, humbug!

Followed by another text.

Yes, Anton, I do know.

He must, Anton thought, find out what 'bah, humbug' meant.

Then he read another text from a couple of months ago that made him smile. But not at her humour, more at how spot-on she had been.

I know it is your weekend off, sorry, but you did say to text with any concerns with any of your patients. Can you happen to be passing by?

Anton had *happened* to be passing by half an hour later and had found Louise sitting on the bed, chatting with the usually sombre Mrs Calini, who was in an unusually elated mood.

'Oh, here's Anton.' Louise had beamed as he had stopped by the bed for a *chat*.

'Anton!' Mrs Calini had started talking in rapid Italian, saying how gorgeous her baby was, just how very, very beautiful he was. Yes, there was nothing specific but Anton had been on this journey with his patient and Louise was right, this was most irregular.

Twelve hours and a lot of investigations later, Mrs Calini had moved from elation to paranoia—loudly declaring that all the other mothers were jealous and likely to steal her beautiful baby. She had been taken up to the psych ward and her infant had remained on Maternity.

Two weeks later the baby had been reunited with Mrs Calini on the psychiatric mother and baby unit and just a month ago they had gone home well.

Anton looked up 'bah, humbug' and soon found out she wasn't talking about odd-looking black and white mints when she used that term.

He read a little bit about Scrooge and how he despised Christmas and started to smile.

Oh, Louise.

God, but he was tempted to text her now, by

accident, of course. In his contacts Louise was there next to 'Labour Ward' after all.

He loathed that she was with Rory but, then again, she had every right to be happy. He'd had his chances over the months and had declined them. So Anton decided against an accidental text to Louise, surprised that he had even considered sending one.

He wasn't usually into games.

He just didn't like that the games had now ended with Louise.

Louise checked her phone the second she awoke, just in case Emily had called or texted her and she'd missed it, but, no, there was nothing.

It had been a very restless night's sleep and it wasn't even five. Louise lay in the dark, wishing she could go back to sleep while knowing it was hopeless.

Instead, she got up and made a big mug of tea and took that back to bed.

Bloody Anton, Louise thought, a little embarrassed at her blatant flirting when she now knew he had the stunning Saffarella to go home to.

Had it all been one-sided?

Louise didn't think so but she gave up torturing herself with it. Anton had always been unavailable to her, even if just emotionally.

After a quick shower Louise blasted her hair with the hairdryer, and as a public service to everyone put some rouge on very pale cheeks then wiped it off because it made her look like a clown.

She took her vitamins and iron and then decided to cheer herself up by wearing the *best* underwear in the world to work today. She had been saving it for the maternity Christmas party but instead she decided to debut it today. It was from the Mistletoe range, the lace dotted with leaves of green and embroidered silk cream berries topped with a pretty red bow—and that was just the panties. The bra was empress line and almost gave her a cleavage, and she loved the little red bow in the middle.

It was far too glamorous for work but, then,

Louise's underwear was always far too glamorous for work.

Instead of having another cup of tea and watching the news, Louise decided to simply go in early and hopefully put her mind at rest by not finding Emily there.

She lived close enough to walk to work. It was very cold so she draped on scarves and walked through the dark and damp morning. It was lovely to step into the maternity unit, which was always nice and warm.

There was Anton sitting sulking at the desk, writing up notes amidst the Naughty Baby Club—comprising all the little ones that had been brought up to the desk to hopefully give their mothers a couple of hours' sleep.

Louise read through the admission board, checking for Emily's name and letting out a breath of relief when she saw that it wasn't there.

'How come you're in early?' she asked Anton, wondering if he was waiting for Emily.

'I couldn't sleep,' Anton said, 'so I thought I'd catch up on some notes.'

They were both sulking, both jealous that the other had had a better night than they'd had.

'I'm going to make some tea,' Louise said. 'Would you like some?'

'Please.' Anton nodded.

'Evie?' Louise asked, and got a shake of the head from the night nurse. 'Tara?'

'No, thanks, we've just had one.'

Louise changed into her scrubs then headed to the kitchen and made herself a nice one, and this time Anton got a hospital teabag.

He knew he was in her bad books with one sip of his tea.

Well, she was in his bad books too.

'You and Rory left very suddenly,' Anton commented. 'I didn't realise that the two of you…'

'We're not on together,' Louise said. 'Well, we were three years ago but we broke up after a few weeks. We're just good friends now.'

'Oh.'

'Rory took me home early last night because I'm worried about Emily,' Louise admitted. She was too concerned about her friend to play games. 'She hasn't called you, has she? You're not here, waiting for her to come in?'

'No.' Anton frowned. 'Why are you worried? She seemed fine last night.'

'She was at first but then she was suddenly tired and went home. Rory said that she'd had a big day at work but…'

'Tell me.'

'She snapped at me and she had that look,' Louise said. 'You know the one…'

'Yep,' Anton said, because, unlike Rory, he did know what Louise meant and he took her concerns about Emily seriously.

'How many weeks is she now?'

'Twenty-seven,' Louise said.

'And how many days…?' Anton asked, pulling Emily's notes up on his computer. 'No, she's twenty-eight weeks today.' Anton read through his notes. 'I saw her last week and all was fine. The pregnancy has progressed normally, just the appendectomy at six weeks.'

'Could that cause problems now?' Louise asked.

'I would have expected any problems from surgery to surface much earlier than this,' Anton said, and he gave Louise a thin smile. 'Maybe she *was* just tired…'

'I'll ring Theatre later and find out what shift she's on,' Louise said. 'In fact, I'll do it now.'

She got put through and was told that Emily was on a late shift today.

'Maybe I am just worrying about nothing,' Louise said.

'Let us hope so.'

A baby was waking up and Tara, a night nurse, was just dashing off to do the morning obs.

'I'll get him.'

Louise picked up the little one and snuggled him in. 'God, I love that smell,' Louise said, inhaling the scent of the baby's hair, then she looked over at Anton.

'Did Saffron have a good night?'

She watched his lips move into a wry smile.

'Not really,' Anton said, and then added, 'And her name is Saffarella.'

'Oh, sorry,' Louise said. 'I got mixed up. Saffron's the one you put in your rice to make it go yellow, isn't it?' Louise corrected herself. 'Expensive stuff, costs a fortune and you only get a tiny—'

'Louise,' Anton warned, 'I don't know quite where you're going there but, please, don't be a bitch.'

'I can't help myself, Anton,' Louise swiftly retorted. 'If you get off with another woman in front of me then you'll see my bitchy side.'

Anton actually grinned; she was so open that she fancied him, so relentless, so *aaagggh*, he thought as he sat there.

'I didn't *get off*, as you say, with Saffarella. We danced.'

'Please,' Louise scoffed.

Maybe he wanted to share the relief he had felt when he had just heard that she and Rory were only friends but, for whatever reason, he put her out of her misery too.

'I took Saffarella back to the hotel she is staying at last night.'

He gave her an inch and, yep, Louise took a mile.

'Really!' Louise gave a delighted grin and covered the baby's ears. 'So you didn't—'

'Louise!'

'The baby can't hear, I've covered his ears. So you and she didn't…?'

'No, we didn't.'

'Did she sulk?' Louise asked with glee, and he grimaced a touch at the memory of the car door slamming.

'Yes.'

'Oh, poor Saffron, I mean Saffarella—now that I know you and she didn't do anything, I can like her.'

They both smiled, though it was with a touch of regret because last night could have been such a nicer night.

'Thanks so much,' Tara said, coming over and looking at the baby. 'He's asleep now, Louise. You can put him back in his isolette.'

'But I don't want to,' Louise said, looking down at the sleeping baby. He was all curled up in her arms, his knees were up and his ankles crossed as if he were still in the womb. His little feet were poking out of the baby blanket and Louise was stroking them.

'They're like kittens' paws,' Louise said, watching his teeny toes curl.

'You are so seriously clucky,' Tara said.

'Oh, I'm more than clucky,' Louise admitted. 'I keep going over to the nativity scene just to pick up Baby Jesus. I have to have one.'

'It will ruin your lingerie career,' Tara warned, but Louise just laughed.

'I'm sure pregnant women can and do wear fabulously sexy underwear—in fact, my agent's going to speak to a couple of companies to see what sort of work they might have for me if I get pregnant.'

'Surely you're missing something if you want a baby…' Tara said, referring to Louise's lack of a love life, but now she had told her mum, now she'd told Rory and Emily knew too, Louise had decided it was time to start to let the world know.

'No, I'm not missing anything.' Louise smiled. 'In fact, I might have to pay a visit to Anton.'

She was referring to the fact she'd found out he was a reproductive specialist too and he gave a wry smile at the ease of her double entendre.

'I have an excellent record,' Anton said.

'So I've heard.' Louise smirked.

Then Anton stopped the joking around and went to get back to his notes. 'You don't need to be rushing. How old are you?'

'Thirty next year!' Louise sighed.

'Plenty of time. You don't have to be thinking about it yet,' Anton said, but it turned out that the ditzy Louise ran deep.

'I think about it a lot,' she admitted. 'In all seriousness, Anton,' she continued, as Tara headed off to do more obs, 'I'm actually confused by the whole thing. I recently saw my GP but she just told me to come off the Pill for a few months.'

Anton frowned, fighting the urge to step in while not wanting to get involved with this aspect of Louise, so he was a little brusque in response. 'The fertility centre at this hospital runs an information night for single women,' Anton offered. 'Your questions would be best answered there.'

'I know they do,' Louise said. 'I've booked in for the next one but it's not till February. That's ages away.'

'It will be here before you know it. As I said, there's no rush.'

'There might be, though,' Louise said, and told him the truth. 'A few years ago I found out I'd probably have problems getting pregnant. That's why I'm off the Pill and trying to sort out my cycle. I know quite a bit but even I'm confused.'

'You need a specialist. Perhaps see an ob/gyn and have him answer your questions, but I would think, from the little you've told me, that you would be referred to a fertility specialist. Certainly, if you are considering pregnancy, you need to get some base bloods down and an ultrasound.'

'Can I come and see you?' Louise was completely serious now. 'Make an appointment, I mean, and then if I did get pregnant…'

'There is a long wait to see me.'

'Even for colleagues?' Louise cheekily checked.

'Especially for colleagues,' Anton said, *really* not liking the way this conversation was going.

'What about privately?' Louise asked, and she was serious about that because all her money from modelling was going into her baby fund.

'Louise.' Anton was even brusquer now. 'Why would you want to be a single mother?'

'I'm sure that's not the first thing you ask your patients when they come to see you,' Louise scolded. 'I don't think that's very PC.'

'But you're not my patient,' Anton pointed out, 'so I don't have to watch what I say. Why would you want to be a single mother?'

'How do you know I'm not in a relationship?' Louise said.

'You just told me that you and Rory were only friends.'

'Hah, but I could have an infertile partner at home.'

'Do you?'

'Lorenzo,' Louise teased, kicking him gently

with her foot. 'And he's very upset that he can't give me babies.'

He knew she was joking, though he refused to smile, and he wanted to capture her foot as she prattled on.

'Or,' Louise continued, 'I might be a lesbian in a very happy relationship and we've decided that we want to have a baby together.' She loved how his lips twitched as she continued. 'I'm the girly one!'

'You're not a very good lesbian,' Anton said, 'given the way that you flirt with me.'

'Ha-ha.' Louise laughed. 'Seriously, Anton—' and she was '—about seeing you privately. You're right, I need to get an ultrasound and some bloods done. I'm going in circles on my own—fertility drugs, artificial insemination or IVF. I'm worried about twins or triplets or even more...' Louise truly was. 'I want someone who knows what they are doing.'

'Of course you do,' Anton agreed. 'If you want, I can recommend someone to you. Richard here is excellent, I can speak with him and give you a referral and get you seen quickly—' Anton started, but Louise interrupted him.

'Why would I see someone else when we both know you're the best?' she pushed. 'Look, I know we mess around…'

'*You* mess around,' Anton corrected.

'Only at work.'

Louise *was* serious, Anton realised. She had that look in her eyes that Anton recognised on women who came to his office. It was a look that said she was determined to get pregnant, so he had no real choice now but to be honest.

No, this conversation wasn't going well for him at all.

'It would be unethical for me to see you,' Anton said, and stood.

'Unethical?' Louise frowned. 'What, because we work together?'

'Professionally unethical,' Anton said, and rolled his eyes as a delighted smile spread across her face. 'I can't say it any clearer than that.'

Ooooh!

She hugged the baby as Anton walked off.

'He *has* got the hots for me,' Louise whispered to the baby, and then let out a loud wolf whistle to Anton's departing back.

No, Anton did not turn around but he did smile.

CHAPTER FIVE

'I NEED SOMEONE to buddy this,' Beth called, and Louise went over to the nurses' station to look at the CTG tracing of one of Beth's patients.

The policy at The Royal was that only two experienced midwives could sign off on a tracing and so a buddy system was in place.

It was way more than a cursory look Louise gave to the tracing. They discussed it for a few moments, going over the recordings of the contractions and foetal heart rate before Louise signed off.

It was a busy morning and it sped by. At lunchtime, as Anton walked into the staffroom, had he had sunglasses then he would have put them on. There was a silver Christmas tree by the television and it was dressed in silver balls. There were silver stars hanging from the ceiling—

really, there was silver everything hanging from every available space.

'Have you been at the tinsel again?' Anton said to Louise, who was eating a tuna salad.

'I have. I just can't help myself. I might have to go and speak with someone about my little tinsel problem—though I took up your suggestion and went with a theme in here!'

'I cannot guess what it was.'

Anton chose to sit well away from her and, for something to do, rather than listen to all the incessant gossip, he picked up a magazine.

Oh, no!

There she was and Louise was right—the underwear was divine.

'Christmas Holly' said the title and there a stunning Louise was in the stockings she'd had on last night but now he got the full effect—bra, stockings and suspenders. Anton turned the page to the Mistletoe range, and the shots, though very lovely and very tasteful, were so sexy that Anton felt his body responding, like some sad old man reading a porn magazine, and he hastily turned to the problem page, just not in time.

Oh, God, he was thinking about swiping the magazine, especially when he glimpsed the Holly and the Ivy shots.

'Ooooh.' Louise looked over and saw what he was reading. 'I'm in that one.' She plucked it from his hands and knelt at the coffee table and turned to the section in the magazine as a little crowd gathered around.

She was so unabashed by it, just totally at ease with her body and its functions in a way that sort of fascinated Anton.

'You've got a cleavage,' Beth said, admiring the shot.

'I know,' Louise said. 'Gorgeous, isn't it?'

'But how?'

Anton closed his eyes. These were women who spent most of their days dealing with breasts and vaginas and they chatted with absolute ease about such things, an ease Anton usually had too, just not when Miss Louise was around.

'Well,' Louise said as Anton stared at the news,

'they take what little I have and sort of squeeze it together and then tape it—there's a lot of scaffolding under that bra,' Louise explained. 'Then they pad the empty part and then they edit out my nipples.'

'Wow!'

'I wish they *were* real,' Louise sighed.

'Would you ever get them done?' Beth asked.

'No,' Louise said, as Anton intently watched the weather report. 'I did think about it one time but, no, I'll stick with what I've been given, which admittedly isn't much. Hopefully they'll be *massive* when I get pregnant and then breast-feed.'

'Anton!' Brenda popped her head in to save the day. 'I've got the husband of one of your patients on the phone. Twenty-eight weeks, back pain...'

'Who?'

'Emily Linton.'

'Merda.' Anton cursed under his breath and then took the phone while trying to ignore Louise, who was now standing over him as Hugh brought him up to speed.

'Okay,' Anton said, as Louise hopped on the spot. 'I'll come down now and meet you at the maternity entrance.'

'Back pain, some contractions,' Anton said. 'Her waters are intact...' As Louise went to follow him out Anton shook his head. 'Maybe Emily needs someone who is not close to her,' Anton said.

'Maybe she needs someone who *is* close to her,' Louise retorted. 'You're not getting rid of me.'

Anton nodded.

'Brenda, can you let the paediatricians know?'

'Of course.'

They stood waiting for the car and Anton looked over. Louise was shivering in the weak winter sun and her teeth were chattering. 'Emily isn't the most straightforward person,' Louise said. 'She acts like she doesn't care when, really, she does.'

Anton nodded and watched as, even though she was terrified for her friend, Louise's lips spread into a wide smile as the car pulled up.

'Come on, trouble,' Louise said, helping her friend into a wheelchair.

'I'm sure it's nothing,' Emily said, as Louise gave directions.

'Hugh, go and park the car and meet us there.'

Once Hugh was out of earshot, Emily let out a little of her fear. 'It's way too soon,' Emily said. Her expression was grim but there were no tears.

'Let's just see where we are,' Anton said.

Though Anton would do his level best to make sure that the pregnancy remained intact, Emily was taken straight through to the delivery ward, just in case.

'I had a bit of a backache last night,' Emily admitted. 'At first I thought it was from standing for so long yesterday. Then, late this morning, I thought I was getting Braxton-Hicks…'

Louise was putting on a foetal monitor as Anton put in an IV line and took some bloods, and then, as Hugh arrived, Anton looked at the tracing. 'The baby is looking very content,' Anton said, and then he put a hand on Emily's stomach as the monitor showed another contraction starting.

'I'm only getting them occasionally,' Emily said.

But sometimes you only needed a few with a baby this small.

'Emily,' Anton said when the contraction had passed, 'I am going to examine you and see where we are.'

But Emily kept panicking, possibly because she didn't *want* to know where they were, and nothing Hugh or Anton might say would reassure her.

'I need you to try and relax,' Anton said.

'Oh, it's so easy for them to say that when they come at you with a gloved hand!' Louise chimed in, and Anton conceded Louise was right to be there because Emily let out a little laugh and she did relax just a touch.

'How long are you here for?' Emily asked Louise, because even though Louise had yesterday told her she was on an early today, clearly such conversations were the last thing on

Emily's mind at the moment and it was obvious that she wanted her friend to be here.

'I've just come on duty,' Louise lied, 'so I'm afraid that you're stuck with me for hours yet.'

Anton examined Emily and Louise passed him a sterile speculum and he took some swabs to check for amniotic fluid and also some swabs to check for any infection.

'You are in pre-term labour,' Anton said. 'You have some funnelling,' Anton explained further. 'Your cervix is a little dilated but if you think of a funnel...' he showed the shape with his hands '...your cervix is opening from the top but we are going to give you medication that will hopefully be able to, if not halt things, at least delay them.' He gave his orders to Louise and she started to prepare the drugs Anton had chosen. 'This should taper off the contractions,' he said as he hooked up the IV, 'and these steroids will help the baby's lungs mature in case it decides to be born. You shall get another dose of these in twenty-four hours.'

Louise did everything she could to keep the

atmosphere nice and calm but it was all very busy. The paediatricians came down and spoke with Anton. NICU was notified that there might be an imminent admission. Anton did an ultrasound and everything on there looked fine. Though the contractions were occasionally still coming, they started to weaken, though Emily had a lot of pain in her back, which was a considerable concern.

'Content,' Anton said again, but this time to the screen. 'Stay in there, little one.'

'And if it doesn't?' Emily asked.

'Then we have everything on hand to deal with that if your baby is born,' Anton said. 'But for now things are settling and what I need for you to do is to lie there and rest.'

'I will,' Emily said. 'First, though, I need a wee.'

'I'll get you a bedpan!' Louise said.

'Please no.'

'I'm afraid so.' Louise smiled. 'Anton's rules.'

Anton smiled as he explained his rules. 'Many say that it makes no difference. If the baby is going to be born then it shall be. Call me old-fashioned but I still prefer that you have complete bed rest, perhaps the occasional shower...'

'Fine.' Emily nodded, perhaps for the first time realising that she was going to be there for a while.

Hugh and Anton waited outside as much laughter came from the room, mainly from Louise, but Emily actually joined in too as they attempted to get a sterile specimen and also to check for a urinary tract infection.

Bedpans were not the easiest things to sit on.

But then Emily stopped laughing. 'Louise, I'm scared if I wee it will come out.'

'You have to wee, Emily,' Louise said, and gave her friend a cuddle. 'And you have to poo and do all those things, but I'm right here.'

It helped to hear that.

'I've got such a bad feeling,' Emily admitted, and Hugh gave a grim smile to Anton as outside they listened to Emily expressing her fears out loud. 'I really do.'

'Okay.' Louise was practical. 'How many women at twenty-eight weeks sit on that bed you're on, having contractions, and say, "I've got a really good feeling"? How many?' Louise asked.

'None.'

'I had a bad feeling last night,' Louise admitted. 'You can ask Anton, you can ask Rory, because I left five minutes after you and I came in early just to look at the board to see if you had been admitted, but I don't have a bad feeling now.'

'Honest?'

'Promise,' Louise said. 'So have a wee.'

'I'm going to give her a sedative,' Anton said to Hugh.

'Won't that relax her uterus?' Hugh checked, and then stopped himself because he trusted Anton.

'I want her to sleep and I want to give her the best chance for those medications to really take hold,' Anton said. 'You saw that her blood pressure was high?'

Hugh nodded—Emily's raised blood pressure could simply be down to anxiety but could also be a sign that she had pre-eclampsia.

'We'll see if there's any protein in her urine,' Anton said. If she did that would be another unwelcome sign that things were not going well.

Louise came out with the bedpan and urine sample, which would be sent to the lab.

'Can you check for protein?' Anton asked.

Louise rolled her eyes at Hugh. 'He thinks that because I'm blonde I'm thick,' she said to a very blond Hugh, who smiled back. 'Of course I'm going to check for protein!'

'He's blondist,' Hugh joked, but then breathed out in relief when Louise called from the pan room.

'No protein, no blood, no glucose—all normal, just some ketones.'

'She hasn't eaten since last night,' Hugh said, which explained the ketones.

'I've put dextrose up but right now the best thing she can do is to rest.'

It was a very long afternoon and evening.

* * *

Louise stayed close by Emily, while Anton delivered two babies but in between checked in on Emily.

At eight, Louise sat and wrote up her notes. It felt strange to be writing about Emily and her baby. She peeled off the latest CTG recording and headed out.

'Can you buddy this?' Louise asked Siobhan, a nurse on labour and delivery this evening.

'Sure.'

They went through the tracing thoroughly, both taking their time and offering opinions before the two midwives signed off.

'It's looking a lot better than before,' Siobhan said. 'Let's hope she keeps improving.'

Around nine-thirty p.m. Anton walked into the womb-like atmosphere Louise had created. The curtains were closed and the room was in darkness and there was just the noise of the baby's heartbeat from the CTG. Emily was asleep and so too was Hugh. Louise sat in a rocking chair, her feet up on a stool, reading a magazine with a clip-on light attached to it that she carried in her pocket for such times, while holding Emily's hand. She let go of the magazine to give a thumb's-up to Anton, and then she put her finger to her lips and shushed him as he walked over to look at the monitors—Louise loathed noisy doctors.

All looked good.

Anton nudged his head towards the corridor and Louise stepped outside and they went into the small kitchenette where all the flower vases were stored and spoke for a while.

'She's still got back pain,' Louise said, and Anton nodded.

'We'll keep her in Delivery tonight but, hopefully, if things continue to improve we can get her onto the ward tomorrow morning.'

'Good.'

'You were right,' Anton said. 'There *was* something going on with her last night.' He saw the sparkle of tears in Louise's eyes because, despite positive appearances, Anton knew she was very worried for her friend.

'I'd love to have been wrong.'

'I know.'

'Anton…' Louise spilled what was on her mind. 'I bought a crib for the baby a few days ago.'

'Okay.'

'It was in a sale and I couldn't resist it. I didn't tell Emily in case she thought it bad luck…'

'Louise!' Anton's firm use of her name told her to let that thought go.

She took a breath.

'Louise,' he said again, and she met his eye. 'That's crazy. I've got Mrs Adams in room two, who's forty-one weeks. She's done everything, the nursery is ready…'

'I know, I know.'

'Just put that out of your mind.'

Louise did. She blew it away then but a tear did sneak out because Louise cared so much about Emily and she was also pretty exhausted. 'Why did it have to be now?' she asked.

'I would love to know that answer,' Anton said, and Louise gave a small smile as he continued. 'It would save me many sleepless nights.'

'I wasn't asking a medical question.'

'I know you weren't.'

Anton stood in the small annexe and looked at Louise. Today she had been amazing, though it wasn't just because she was Emily's friend. Every mother got Louise's full attention. It was wrong of him to compare her to Dahnya, Anton realised. It was futile to keep going back to that terrible day.

Louise was too worried about Emily to notice his silence and she rattled on with her fears.

'I know twenty-eight weeks isn't tiny tiny but…'

'It is far too soon,' Anton agreed. 'She's *just* into her third trimester but we'll do all we can to prolong it. It looks like we've just bought her another day and those steroids are in. The night staff have arrived, Evie is on and she is very good.'

Louise nodded. 'I know she is but I'm going to sleep here tonight.'

'Go home,' Anton said, because Louise really

did look pale, but she shook her head at his suggestion. 'Louise, you have been here since six.'

'And so have you,' Louise pointed out. 'I didn't think you were on call tonight, Anton, so what's your excuse for being here?'

'I'll be a lot happier by morning. I just want to be close if something occurs.'

'Well, I'm the same. If something happens tonight then I want to be here with Emily.'

'I get that but—Louise, I never thought I'd say this to you, but you look awful.'

It was a rather backhanded compliment but it did make her smile. 'I'll go and lie down soon,' Louise said, and looked over as Hugh came out.

'Is she awake?'

'Yes, they're just doing her obs. Thanks for today,' Hugh said to them both. 'I'm going to text and ring five thousand people now. Emily told her mum and, honestly, it's spread like wildfire...'

'I get it,' Louise said, because she knew about Emily's very complex family and the last thing she needed now was the hordes arriving. 'I've put her down as no visitors.'

'Thanks for that,' Hugh said. 'I'm going to ring for pizza—do you want some?'

'No, thanks.' Louise shook her head and yawned. 'I'm going to go and sleep.'

'Anton?'

'Sounds good.'

Louise handed over to Evie, the night nurse who would be taking care of Emily. 'Promise, promise, promise that you'll come and get me if anything happens.'

'Promise.'

'I'm going to take a pager,' Louise said, 'just in case you're too busy, so if you page him…' she nodded to Anton '…page me too.'

Louise went to the hotbox and took out one of the warm blankets that they covered newly delivered mums in. Brenda would freak if she knew the damage that Louise singlehandedly did to the laundry budget but she was too cold and tired to care about that right now.

'I'll be in the store cupboard if anything happens.'

'Store cupboard?' Anton said.

'Where all the night nurses sleep.' Louise nodded to the end of the corridor. ''Night, guys. 'Night, Hugh. I'll just go and say night to Emily if she's awake.'

She popped in and there was Emily half-awake as Evie fiddled with her IV.

'You've done so well today.' Louise smiled, standing wrapped in her blanket. 'I'm just going to get some shut-eye but I'm just down the hall, though I have a feeling I shan't be needed.'

'Thanks so much for staying,' Emily said.

'Please.' Louise gave her a kiss goodnight on her forehead. 'Hopefully we'll move you to a room tomorrow. I'm going to have a jiggle with the beds in the morning and give you one of the nice ones.' She spoke then in a loud whisper. 'One of the private ones!'

'You're such a bad girl.' Evie smiled.

'I know.' Louise grinned. 'Sleep!' Louise said

to Emily and then stroked her stomach. 'And you, little one, stay in there.'

'Do you know what I'm having?' Emily asked, and Louise just smiled as Emily spoke on. 'Hugh knows and when I said that I didn't want to find out, he said that he wouldn't tell me even if I begged him.'

'Do you want to know?' Louise asked.

'No, yes, no,' Emily admitted. 'But I want to know if you know.'

'I do,' Louise said, and then burst into Abba. '"I do, I do, I do, I do, I do,"' Louise sang, just as Anton and Hugh walked in. 'But I'm not telling. If you want to know you can speak to Anton.'

'She's mad,' Emily said, when Louise had gone but she said it in the nicest way.

'Completely mad,' Anton agreed. 'How are you feeling now?'

'A bit better.'

'Any questions?' Anton checked, but Emily shook her head.

'I think you've answered them all. Presumably you know what I'm having?'

'Of course I do,' Anton said. 'You know you are allowed to change your mind and find out if you want to.'

'I want it to be a surprise.'

'Then a surprise it will be.'

'Are you going home now?' Emily asked, because she had been told he was only here till six and she felt both guilty and relieved when Anton shook his head.

'Stephanie is the on-call obstetrician tonight and she will be keeping an eye on you so that I can get some rest as I am working tomorrow. I am staying here tonight, though, and if anything changes, I have asked her to discuss it with me.'

'Thank you.'

The store cupboard was actually an empty four-bedded ward at the front of the unit and was used to store beds, trolleys, stirrups, birth balls and all that sort of stuff. Louise curled up on one of the beds and lay there with her eyes closed, hoping that they would stay that way till morning.

She was exhausted, she'd barely had any sleep last night, but now that she finally could sleep, Louise simply could not relax. There was that knot of worry about Emily and another knot between her legs when she thought about Anton and the fact that he actually liked her.

In *that* way!

After half an hour spent growing more awake by the minute Louise padded out with her blanket around her.

Anton gave her a smile and she couldn't really remember him smiling like that, unless to a patient. In fact, he didn't smile like *that* to the patients.

'Food should be here soon,' Anton said.

Louise shook her head and instead of waiting for the pizza to arrive she had a bowl of cornflakes in the kitchen. Anton looked up as she returned with a bottle of sparkling water and a heat pack for her cramping stomach and then took two painkillers.

She tossed her now cold blanket into the linen skip and took out a newly warm one.

'If Brenda knew…' Anton warned, because the cost of laundering a blanket was posted on many walls, warning staff to use them sparingly.

'I like to be warm at night,' Louise said, and, no, she hadn't meant it to be provocative but from the look that burnt between them it was.

She headed back to the storeroom but sleep still would not come.

Then she heard the slam of the door. Louise climbed out of the bed to tell whoever it was off for doing that but then a delicious scent reached her nose.

Pizza.

OMG.

She could almost taste the pepperoni.

Louise hadn't said no to Anton because of some diet, she had said no because…

Well.

Because.

No, she did not want to be huddled up at the desk with him—she might, the way she was feeling this moment, very possibly end up licking his face.

God, he was hot.

Her stomach was growling, though, and it was the scent of pizza that was at fault, not her, Louise decided as she smiled and pulled out her phone.

Anton had two phones and one of the numbers she was privy to. It was his work phone and she'd call him on it at times if one of his patients weren't well while he was off duty, or she might text him sometimes for advice.

She wondered if he'd tell her off for using it for something so trivial.

Or if he'd ignore her request, perhaps?

Anton sat eating pizza as Hugh fired off texts to family to let them know that Emily was doing well.

When his work phone buzzed, indicating a text, Anton read it and decided it might be best to ignore it.

For months he had done his best to ignore her yet since he'd see her up that stepladder it had been a futile effort at best.

He did try to ignore it. In fact, he said goodnight to Hugh and then went into the on-call room, grimly determined to sleep.

Then he read her text again and gave up fighting. He went back to the desk, picked up two slices of pizza and headed off to where perhaps he shouldn't.

CHAPTER SIX

'PIZZA MAN!' ANTON said, as he came into the dark room.

'Oh, my, and an authentic Italian one too!' Louise smiled in the dark and sat up and then took out her light from her pocket and shone it up at him. 'And so good looking.'

'You changed your mind about the pizza?'

'I did,' Louise said. 'A bowl of cornflakes wasn't going to cut it tonight.'

'I could have told you that half an hour ago— you need to eat more.'

'I do eat.'

Anton shook his head very slowly. 'With my sister's line of work I know all the tricks, *all* of them,' Anton said. 'Tell me the truth.'

'Okay, I do watch my weight,' Louise admitted, 'a lot! But I am not anorexic.'

'I can see that you're not anorexic but you do seem to live off salad.'

'Ah, so you notice what I eat, Anton, how sweet!' Louise teased, and then she answered him properly. 'I love my modelling work,' Louise said. 'I mean I *love* it and it is my job to present at a certain weight but I don't do the dangerously thin stuff. Yes, for the most part I have to watch what I eat but, in saying that, I eat very well. I'm nearly thirty. I can't believe I'm still working…'

'I can.' Anton smiled.

'Anyway, I've got a huge photo shoot on Christmas Eve,' Louise explained, as she ate warm pizza. 'It's for Valentine's Day and I'm going to pay a small fortune to get dressed up to the nines and have my hair and make-up done so, yes, I'm being careful.' Her slice of pizza was finished and he handed her the other one. 'I'm just not being very careful tonight.'

'If you are looking at trying for a baby…'

'I would never jeopardise that for work, Anton.

I'm just eating healthily. What happened this morning is unrelated to that.'

'Good to know.'

He glanced at the stirrups over the bed. 'You really sleep here?'

'Of course,' Louise said, and then she looked to where his gaze fell. 'Do you want me in stirrups, Anton?'

He actually laughed. 'No. It is that I *don't* want you in stirrups that means you can't be my patient.' He explained as best he could. 'Louise, I know I have given mixed messages. Yes, I like you but I never wanted to get involved with someone at work.'

'We're not at work.' Louise smiled a provocative smile. 'Officially we're both off duty.'

'Louise, the thing is—'

'Please, please, don't,' Louise said. 'Please spare me the lecture, because, guess what, I'm the same. The last thing I want now is a full-on relationship, particularly with you.'

Anton frowned in slight surprise. He'd come in having finally given in and deciding that they should perhaps give it a go, only to find out that a relationship with him was far from her mind.

'Why *particularly* not with me?'

'Okay, I think you're as sexy as hell and occasionally funny but I think you'd be very controlling, and that's fine in the bedroom perhaps—'

'I am not controlling,' Anton immediately interrupted. 'Well, I know that I am at work but not when I'm in a relationship.'

'Oh, they all say that.' Louise put on an Italian accent. 'I do not want my woman posing in her underwear…'

'That is the worst Italian accent ever.' He frowned at her opinion of him. 'I happen to think your work is very beautiful.'

'Really?'

'Of course it is.' He was still frowning. 'Have you had trouble in the past—?'

'I have,' Louise said quickly, hurrying over that part of her life, 'and so I keep things on my terms. The only thing I want to focus on right now is myself and becoming a mum. I'm not on a husband shop.'

A flirt, some fun, was all she was prepared to give to a man right now.

Though she had fancied Anton for ages.

Ages.

Pizza done, Louise went into her pocket, peeled off some baby wipes from a small packet she carried and wiped her hands. Then she went into her pockets again and pulled out a breath spray.

'What the hell have you got in those pockets?'

'Many, many things—basically my pockets are designed so that I don't have to get up if I'm comfy.' Louise smiled and settled back on the pillow. 'The breath spay is so that I don't submit a labouring woman to my pizza breath, and,' she added, 'it's also terribly convenient if you want to kiss me goodnight.'

'Louise,' Anton warned. 'We're not going to be skulking around in the shadows.'

'I know,' Louise sighed regretfully. 'How come you left fertility?' She yawned, but was pleased when Anton sat on the edge of the bed.

'I missed obstetrics,' Anton admitted, though he too chose to avoid the dark stuff.

'Is it nice to be back doing it?'

'Some days,' Anton said, 'like yesterday with Hannah's son—that was a really good day. Today...' He thought for a moment. 'Yes, it is still good. Thanks for your help today, you were right to stay—it is good for Emily to have you nearby.'

'You're making me nervous, Anton—you're being too nice.'

Anton smiled and watched as she put her hand under the blanket and turned the hot pack on her stomach.

'Still hurt?'

'Yep.'

He wanted his hand there.

Louise wanted the same thing.

She wanted him to lean forward and Anton actually felt as if her hand were at the back of his head, dragging him down, but it wasn't her hand that was pressuring him, it was want.

'I'm going to go,' Anton said. 'I just wanted to clear the air.'

'It doesn't feel very clear,' Louise said, because it was thick with sexual tension, a tension that had come to a head last night but had had no outlet for either of them.

'You're right, it doesn't,' Anton agreed. 'You are such a flirt, Louise,' he said, his mouth approaching hers.

'I know.' She smiled then asked a question as his lovely mouth approached. 'If you were intending to just pop in to clear the air, why did you brush your teeth before you came in?'

'I was *hoping* to clear the air but you have worn me down.'

They were far from worn down as their mouths finally met. It was supposed to break the tension but instead it upped it as, in the dark, Louise found out how lovely that sulky mouth could be.

The mixture of soft lips and rough stubble had her break on contact.

Anton had decided on one small kiss to chase away a wretched day but small was relative,

Anton told himself as he slipped in his tongue and met the caress of hers, for it was still a small kiss if he compared it to the one he really wanted to give.

For Louise, it was bliss. She could not remember a kiss that had been nicer, and her hands moved up to his head and their kiss deepened from intimate to provocative. As he moved to remove her hands and halt things he changed his mind as his thumb grazed her breast. Anton heard the purr and the nudge of her body into his palm, like a cat demanding attention, and so he stroked her through the fabric, until for both of them he had to feel her.

Anton went to lift her top, just to get to her breast, but the heat pack slipped off and she willed his hand to change direction, her tongue urging him on as Anton obliged.

He could feel the ball of tension of her uterus as his hand slipped down instead of up, stroking her tense stomach as he kissed her more deeply.

Louise lifted her knees to the bliss and the sensation but then she peeled her mouth from his.

'Anton…'

'I know that you do,' he said, not caring a bit. 'What colour underwear?' he asked, as he toyed with the lace.

'Cream and green, with a red bow—it's from the Mistletoe collection.'

She loved his moan in her mouth and the feel of his fingers creeping lower. His warm palm massaged low on her stomach as his finger hit the spot and Louise felt her face become red and hot as she kissed now his neck then his ears. One of his hands was behind her head, supporting it, while beneath the other she succumbed.

The tension hit and his mouth suckled hers as he stroked her through the deepest come of her life and then she felt the bliss abate as her stomach lay soft beneath his palm. Her intimate twitches stilled and Louise lay quiet for a moment.

'Better?' Anton asked.

'Positively sedated.'

She lay in sated bliss, pain free for the first time today, and trying to tell herself it was just the sex she wanted as she moved her hand and stroked his thick erection.

'Poor Anton,' she said.

'There have been way too many poor Antons of late,' Anton said. 'I'm going to go and you're going to sleep and—'

'We never discuss this again.' Louise smiled. 'Got it!'

How was she supposed to sleep after that? Louise thought as Anton made his way out.

It took about forty-seven seconds!

CHAPTER SEVEN

LOUISE AWOKE TO the sound of the domestic's floor polisher in the hallway and the even happier sound of no pager, which meant nothing had happened with Emily and so she padded out to the ward.

'How is she?' Louise asked Evie.

'Very good,' Evie said. 'She's slept mostly through and her back ache has eased and the contractions have stopped.' She looked at Louise, who was yawning. 'Why don't you go home?'

'I'm going to have a shower and then I'll see Emily over to her room before I do just that.'

'Well, the royal suite is empty.' Evie smiled as she used the name they all called it. 'I'll go and set it up.'

'I'll do that when I've had my shower,' Louise said, smiling when she heard Anton's voice.

'Morning, Louise,' Anton said, looking all the more handsome for not having shaven. 'How did you sleep?'

'Oh, I went out like a light,' Louise answered. She headed off to the shower and had to wash with the disinfectant soap used for washing hands. Smelling like a bathroom cleaner commercial, she headed out to set up the room for Emily.

It was hardly a royal suite but it had its own loo and was more spacious than others and there was a trundle bed if Hugh wanted to stay. Louise checked the oxygen and suction and that there were pads and vomit bowels and suchlike.

Anton checked in on Emily and was very happy with her lack of progress and agreed that she could be moved.

'Every day that you don't go into labour is a good day,' Anton said, as Louise helped her onto the bed. 'For now you are on strict bed rest and that means bedpans.'

'Okay.' Emily nodded. She wasn't going to argue if it meant her baby stayed put. 'I feel much more positive today.' She looked over at Louise. 'You can go home now.'

'I am,' Louise said. 'But you're to text me with anything you want me to bring in for you. I can visit tonight or tomorrow. I'm off for two days now but—'

'I'll text you,' Emily interrupted, because Louise lived by her phone and they texted each other most days anyway.

As they headed out—Anton to start his shift, Louise to commence her days off—he asked if he could have a word with her in his office.

'Sure,' Louise said.

She knew what was coming and immediately she broached it. 'Don't worry, I get that last night was an aberration.' She saw him frown. 'A one-off.'

Anton wasn't so sure. He had no regrets about last night and he looked at the woman standing before him and wanted to get to know her some more, but before he did there was something that he first needed to know.

'This referral, are you sure that now is the right time?'

'Very sure,' Louise said. 'I've been thinking about it for close to a year.'

'Okay...' Anton said, because that alone was enough for him to ensure last night remained an *aberration*, although still he would like to give them a chance. 'Why don't you wait a while? Maybe we can—?'

'Anton, I already have waited a while. I'm twenty-nine years old and for twenty-eight of those years I have wanted a baby. I didn't just dress up my dollies and put them in a pram, Anton, I used to put them up my dress...' Anton smiled as she carried on. 'I'm not brilliant at relationships.'

'Why would you say that?'

'Oh, I've gathered quite a list of the reasons over the years.' Louise started to tick off on her fingers. 'I'm high maintenance, vain, obsessed with having a baby, inappropriate at times...I could go on but you get the drift. And, yes, I am all of those things and shall happily continue to be them. But, while relationships may not be my forte, I do know for a fact that I shall be a brilliant mum. So many women do it themselves these days.'

'Even so...'

'It's not a decision I've come to lightly. I've sat on it for close to a year and so, if I could have that referral, it would be completely brilliant.'

He wrote one out for her there and then. 'I'll let his secretary know this morning. When you call ask to speak to her because Richard is very booked up too.'

'Thank you.'

'Louise...'

'Anton.' She turned round. She did not want to hear now how they might stand a chance, and she did not want to be put off her dream. One of the reasons she was attracted to him perhaps was that he had been so unobtainable and she wanted that to remain the same. 'Don't be such a girl!'

Six feet two of testosterone stood there and smiled as she continued.

'It was fun, there can be more fun, just as long

as it's conducted well away from work, but I *am* going ahead with this.'

He said nothing as she stepped out and Louise didn't really want him to. She didn't want to hear that maybe they could give it a go. She had fancied him for ever, since the moment she had first laid eyes on him, and now, when the year she had given herself to come to her decision was almost up, when her dream was in sight, Anton was suddenly interested.

Why couldn't he have left it at sex?

That, Louise could deal with.

It was the relationship part that terrified her.

Louise went and visited her family that morning and told them what was going on with Emily. When she got home Emily texted, asking her to go shopping for some nightwear but that there was no rush. And she added…

Something suitable, Louise!!!

Louise killed a couple of happy hours choosing nightwear for a pregnant, soon-to-be breastfeeding woman, while pretending she was shopping for herself. She did her level best to buy not what she'd like but what she guessed Emily would like, and, finally home, she thought about Anton and what had happened.

Not just their kiss and things, more the revelation that he liked her.

She had always been herself with him. Almost, since the day they had met, she had actually *practised* being herself with him. Anton had no idea just how much he had helped her. Not once had he told her to tone it down as she'd gradually returned to the woman she once had been.

She didn't particularly want Anton to know just how bad things had been. In fact, as her fingers traced the scar on her scalp and her tongue slid over the crown on her front tooth, she could not imagine telling him what had happened in her past—it would be a helluva lot to dump on him.

Louise let out a breath as she recalled her family's and friends' reactions.

It had been Emily she had called on Boxing Day and Rory too.

Rory, whose friendship she had dumped, had, when she'd needed him, patched her up enough to go and face her parents at least.

No, she did not even want to think of Anton's reaction to her tale so she pushed all thoughts of that away and pulled out the referral letter and made the call she had been waiting for ever to make.

Anton must have rung ahead as promised because when Louise spoke to the secretary she was told that there had been a cancellation and that she could see Richard the following Wednesday at ten a.m. Louise checked her diary on her phone and saw that she was on a late that day.

Perfect!

Louise put down the phone and did a little happy dance.

Finally, possibly, her baby was on the way!

CHAPTER EIGHT

EVERY QUESTION THAT Louise had, and there were many, was answered.

Susan had come to Louise's appointment with her and Louise was very glad to have her mother by her side. She knew she would probably forget half of what was said later. Also it was easier if her mother understood what was happening first hand.

Richard ordered a full screening, along with a pelvic ultrasound, and did a thorough examination, as well as looking through the app she had on her phone that charted all her dates.

'We have counsellors here and I really suggest that you take up my suggestion and make an appointment. The next step is to await all the blood results and then I'll see you in the new year and we'll look at the ways we can go ahead.'

Louise nodded.

'But you think I'll probably end up having IVF?' Louise said, because that was the impression she had got during the consultation. She was nervous that the fertility drugs might produce too many eggs but with IVF it was more controlled and Louise only wanted one embryo put back. Richard had even discussed egg sharing, which would give Louise one round of IVF free.

'I'm leaning that way, given your irregular cycle and that you want to avoid a multiple pregnancy, but right now I'd suggest you carry on with the iron and folic acid till we get the results back. We might put you on something stronger once they're in. For now, go and have a good Christmas.'

Louise made an appointment for the second week in January, when Richard returned from his Christmas break, and she made an appointment for an ultrasound and then went and had all the bloodwork done as well.

'Aren't you going to book the counsellor?' Susan asked.

'Why would I need to see one?' Louise said. 'You didn't have to see one before you had your three children.'

'True,' Susan responded, 'but before we went in you said that you were going to do *everything* he suggests.'

'And I am,' Louise said, 'apart from that one.'

Louise's cheeks were unusually pink as they walked down the corridor. Her mind was all ajumble because even as little as a couple of weeks ago she'd have happily signed up to talk to someone. She was one hundred per cent sure that she wanted this.

Or make that ninety-nine point nine per cent positive.

'Have you got time for a quick lunch before your shift?' Susan asked.

She did have time but unfortunately that point one per cent, or rather Anton, was already in the canteen and Louise was very conscious of him as they got their meals. Fortunately the table that Susan selected was quite far away from where Anton sat.

'Well, all I can say is that he was a lot better than the GP,' Susan said. 'Do you feel better for having seen him?'

'I do.'

'You're very quiet all of a sudden.'

Louise didn't know whether or not to say anything to her mum.

Actually, she didn't know if there even was anything to discuss. She and Anton had returned to business as usual after the other night. She was being far less flirtatious and Anton was checking up on her work even more than usual, if that was possible.

'I think I like someone, Mum,' Louise admitted. 'I'm a bit confused, to be honest.'

'Does he know that you like him?'

Louise nodded. 'And he also knows I'm doing this but I think if I continue to go ahead then it takes away any chance for us. I don't even know if I want us to have a chance.'

Susan asked what should have been a simple question. 'What's he like?'

'I don't really know.' Louise gave a wry laugh.

'I know what he's like at work and I find him a bit…' She hesitated. 'Well, he's very thorough with his patients and I'm pretty used to doctors dismissing and overriding midwives…' Louise thought for a long moment before continuing. 'I've just fancied him for a long time but nothing ever happened and now, when I've decided to do this, he seems to want to give us a try.'

'How long have you liked him for?' Susan asked.

'About six months.'

'And if he'd tried anything six months ago, what would you have done?'

'Run a mile.'

'If he'd tried anything three months ago, what would you have done?'

'Run a mile,' Louise admitted.

Only now was she truly healing.

'Do you want to give it a try?'

'I think so,' Louise said, 'but I want this so much too.'

She wanted back her one hundred per cent and her unwavering certainty she was finally on the right path. Unthinkingly she looked across the canteen and possibly the cause of her indecision sensed it, because Anton glanced over and briefly met her gaze.

'I don't see a problem.' Susan picked up her knife and fork and brought Louise back to the conversation. 'You don't have an appointment till the second week of January and Richard did say to go and enjoy Christmas. Have some fun, heaven knows, you deserve it. Maybe just try not to think about getting pregnant for a few weeks.'

Louise nodded, though her heart wasn't in it. Her mum tried, she really did, but she simply couldn't get it. Getting pregnant wasn't something Louise could shove in a box and leave in her wardrobe and drag it out in a few weeks and pick up again— it was something she had been building towards for a very long time.

She glanced over and saw that Anton was walking out of the canteen. There had been so little conversation of late between them that Susan could never have guessed the topic of their conversation had just walked past them.

'Think about counselling,' Susan suggested again.

'Why would I when I've got you?' Louise smiled.

'Ah, but since when did you tell me all that's going on?'

Her mother was right, she didn't tell her parents everything. 'Maybe I will,' Louise said, because this year had been one of so many changes. Even as little as a month or so ago she'd have died on the spot had Anton responded to one of her flirts. She was changing, ever changing, and every time she felt certain where she was heading, the road seemed to change direction again.

No.

Louise refused to let go of her dream.

'I need to get to my shift.'

'And I need to hit the shops.' Susan smiled. 'Come over at the weekend, I'll make your favourite.'

'I shall,' Louise said, and gave her mum a kiss goodbye. 'I'll give you a call. Thanks for coming with me today.'

* * *

Louise's patient allocation was a mixed bag between Stephanie and Anton's patients and all were prenatal patients, which meant no baby fix for Louise this shift.

'Hi, Carmel, I'm Louise,' she introduced herself to a new patient. Carmel had been admitted via the antenatal clinic where she had been found to have raised blood pressure. 'How are you?'

'Worried,' Carmel said. 'I thought I was just coming for my antenatal appointment and I find out my blood pressure's high and that the baby's still breech. I'm trying to sort out the other children.'

'This is your third?'

Carmel nodded. 'I've got a three- and a five-year-old. My husband really doesn't have any annual leave left and I can't ask my mum.' Carmel started to cry and, having taken her blood pressure, Louise sat on the chair by her bed.

'There's still time for the baby to turn,' Louise

said. 'You're not due till January...' she checked her notes '...the seventh.'

'But Stephanie said if it doesn't turn then I'll have a Caesarean before Christmas.'

Louise nodded because, rather than the chance of the mother going into spontaneous labour, Caesareans were performed a couple of weeks before the due date.

'I just can't be here for Christmas. I know the baby might have come then anyway but at least with a natural labour I could have had a chance to be in and out...' Carmel explained what was going on a little better. 'My mum's really ill— it's going to be her last Christmas.'

Poor Carmel had so much going on in her life at the moment that hospital was the last place she wanted to be. Right now, though, it was the place she perhaps needed to be, to concentrate on the baby inside and let go a little. Louise sat with her for ages, listening about Carmel's mum's illness and all the plans they had made for Christmas Day that were now in jeopardy.

Finally, having talked it out, Carmel calmed

a bit and Louise pulled the curtains and suggested she sleep. 'I'll put a sign on the door so that you're not disturbed.'

'Unless it's my husband.'

'Of course.' Louise smiled. 'The sign just says to speak to the staff at the desk before coming in.'

She checked in on Felicity, who was one of Anton's high-risk pregnancies, and then she got to Emily.

'How's my favourite patient?' Louise asked a rather grumpy Emily.

Emily was very bored, very worried and also extremely uncomfortable after more than a week and a half spent in bed. She was relying heavily on Louise's chatter and humour to keep her from the dark hole that her mind kept slipping into. 'I'm dying to hear how you got on at your appointment.'

'It went really well,' Louise said, as she took Emily's blood pressure.

'Tell me.'

'He was really positive,' Louise explained,

'though not in a false hope sort of way, just really practical. I'm going to be seeing him in the new year, when all my results are in, to see the best direction to take, but I think it will be IVF.'

'Really!'

'I think so.' Louise nodded. 'He discussed egg sharing, which would mean I'll get a round of IVF free...'

'You don't feel funny about egg sharing?' Emily asked, just as Anton walked in.

'God, no,' Louise said, happy to chat on. 'I'd love to be able to help another woman to get her baby. It would be a win-win situation. I think egg sharing is a wonderful thing.'

She glanced over as Anton pulled out the BP cuff.

'I've done Emily's blood pressure,' Louise said.

'I'm just checking it for myself.'

Louise gritted her jaw. He did this all the time, *all the time*, even more so than before, and though it infuriated Louise she said nothing.

Here wasn't the place.

'Everything looks good,' Anton said to Emily. 'Twenty-nine weeks and four days now. You are doing really well.'

'I'm so glad,' Emily said, 'but I'm also so...' Emily didn't finish. 'I hate that I'm complaining when I'm so glad that I'm still pregnant.'

'Of course you are bored and fed up.' Anton shrugged. 'Would a shower cheer you up?'

'Oh, yes.'

'Just a short one,' Anton said, 'sitting on a chair.'

'Thank you,' Emily said, but when Anton had gone she looked at Louise. 'What's going on with you two?'

'Nothing,' Louise said.

'Nothing?' Emily checked. 'Come on, Louise, it's me. I'm losing my mind here. At least you can tell me what's going on in the real world.'

'Maybe a teeny tiny thing *has* gone on,' Louise said, 'but we're back to him sulking at me now and double-checking everything that I do.'

'Please, Louise, tell me what has happened between you.'

'Nope,' Louise said, but then relented a touch. 'We got off with each other a smudge but I think the big chill is from my getting IVF.'

'Well, it wouldn't be the biggest turn-on.'

'I guess.'

'Can you put it off?'

'I don't want to put it off,' Louise said. 'Then again, I sort of do.' She was truly confused. 'God, could you imagine being in a relationship with Anton? He'd be coming home and checking I'd done hospital corners on the bed and things...'

'He's nothing like that,' Emily said.

'Ah, but you get his hospital bedside manner.'

'Why not just try?'

'Because I've sworn off relationships, they never work out... I don't know,' Louise sighed, and then she looked at her friend and told her the truth. 'I'm scared to even try.'

'When's the maternity do?' Emily asked.

'Friday, but I'm on a late shift, so I'll only catch the end.'

'If you get changed at work I want to see you before you go.'

'You will.' Louise gave a wicked smile. 'Let's see if he can rustle up another supermodel.'

'Or?'

Louise didn't answer the question because she didn't know the answer herself. 'I'll go and set up the shower for you,' Louise said instead, and opened Emily's locker and started to get her toiletries out. 'What do you want to wear?'

'Whatever makes me look least like a prostitute,' Emily said, because, after all, it was Louise who had shopped for her!

'But you look gorgeous in all of them,' Louise said, 'and I promise that you're going to feel gorgeous too once you've had a shower.'

Emily actually did. After more than a week of washing from a bowl, a brief shower and a hair wash had her feeling so refreshed that she actually put on some make-up and her smile matched the scarlet nightdress that Louise had bought her.

'Wrong room!' Hugh joked, when he dropped in during a lull between patients, please to see how much brighter Emily looked.

In fact, Emily had quite a lot of visitors and Anton glanced into her room as he walked past.

'Is she resting?' Anton asked Louise.

'I'm going to shoo them out soon,' Louise said. 'She's had her sister and mum and now Hugh's boss and his wife have dropped in.'

Alex and Jennifer were lovely, just lovely, but Emily really did need her rest and so, after checking in on Carmel, who seemed much calmer since her sleep and a visit from her husband and children, Louise popped in on Emily, dragging the CTG monitor with her.

'How are you?' Louise asked.

'Fine!' Emily said, but she had that slightly exhausted look in her eyes as she smiled brightly.

'That's good.' Louise turned to the visitors. She knew Alex very well from the five years she had worked in Theatre and she knew Jennifer a little too. 'I'm sorry to be a pain, but I've got to pop Louise on the monitor.'

'Of course,' Jennifer said. 'We were just leaving.'

'Don't rush,' Louise said, while meaning the opposite. 'I'm just going to get some gel.'

That would give them time to say goodbye.

Of course Emily was grateful for visitors but even a shower, after all this time in bed, was draining, and Louise would do everything and anything she had to do to make sure Emily got her rest. By the time she returned with the gel Alex and Jennifer had said their goodbyes and were in the corridor.

'How are you, Louise?' Alex asked. 'Missing Theatre?'

'A bit,' Louise admitted, 'although I simply love it here.'

'Well, we miss you,' Alex said kindly, and then glanced over to the nurses' station, where Anton was writing his notes. 'Oh, there's Anton. Jennifer, I must introduce you—'

'Not now, darling,' Jennifer said. 'We really do have to get home for Josie.'

'It will just take two minutes.' Alex was insistent but as he went to walk over, Jennifer caught his arm.

'Alex, I really am tired.'

'Of course.' Alex changed his mind and they wished Louise goodnight before heading off the ward.

Louise looked at Anton, remembering the night of the theatre do and Anton's stilted response when Alex had said he hadn't yet met his wife. Even if she and Anton were trying to keep their distance a touch, Louise couldn't resist meddling.

'She's gone,' Louise said, as he carried on writing.

'Who?'

'Jennifer.'

'That's good.'

'She's nice, isn't she?' Louise said, and watched his pen pause for a second.

'So I've heard,' Anton responded, and carried on writing.

'Have you met her?'

Anton looked up and met Louise's eyes, which were sparkling with mischief. 'Should I have?'

'I don't know.' Louise smiled, all the more curious, but, looking at him, properly looking at him for the first time since he had handed her the referral, she was curious now for different reasons. 'Why aren't we talking, Anton?'

'We're talking now.'

'Why are you checking everything I do?'

'I'm not.'

'Believe me, you are. I might just as well give you the obs trolley and follow you around and simply write your findings down.'

'Louise, I like to check my patients myself. It has nothing to do with you.'

'Okay.' She went to go but changed her mind. 'We're not talking, though, are we?'

He glanced at the sticking plaster on her arm from where she had had blood tests. 'How was your appointment?'

'He was very informative,' Louise said.

'You're seeing him again?'

'In January.' Louise nodded.

'May I ask…?' Anton said, and Louise closed her eyes.

'Please don't.'

'So I just sit here and say nothing?' Anton checked.

He glanced down the corridor. 'Come to my office.'

Louise did as she wanted to hear what he had to say.

'I want to see if we can have a chance and I don't think we'll get one with you about to go on IVF.'

'Oh, so I'm to put all my plans on hold because you now think we might have a chance.'

'I don't think that's unreasonable.'

'I do,' Louise said. 'I very much do. I've liked you for months,' she said, 'months and months, and now, when I'm just getting it together, when I'm going ahead with what I've decided to do, you suddenly decide, oh, okay, maybe I'll give her a try.'

'Come off it, Louise…'

'No, you come off it,' Louise snapped back. A part of her knew he was right but the other part of her knew that she was. She'd cancelled her dreams for a man once before and had sworn never to do it again and so she went to walk off.

'You won't even discuss it?'

'I need to think,' Louise said.

'Think with me, then.'

'No.'

She was scared to, scared that he might make up her mind, and she was so past being that person. Instead, she gave him a cheeky smile. 'Richard told me to have a *very* nice Christmas.'

Her smile wasn't returned.

'I'm not into Christmas.'

'I meant—'

'I know what you meant, Louise,' Anton said. 'You want some gun for hire.'

'Ooh, Anton!' Louise smiled again and then thought for a moment. 'Actually, I do.'

'Tough.'

Anton stood in his office for a few moments as she walked off.

Maybe he'd been a bit terse there, he conceded.

But it was hearing Louise talk about egg sharing with Emily that had had him on edge. From the little Louise had told him about her fertility issues he had guessed IVF would be her best option if she wanted to get pregnant. Often women changed their minds after the first visit. He had hoped it might be the case with Louise while deep down knowing that it wouldn't be.

He had seen her sitting in the canteen with her mother today—and it had to have been her mum as Anton could see where Louise had got her looks from—but even that had caused disquiet.

Louise had talked this through with her family. It was clearly not a whim.

It just left no room for them.

Anton wanted more than just sex for a few weeks.

Then he changed his mind because a few weeks of straight sex sounded pretty ideal right now.

Perhaps they should try pushing things aside and just seeing how the next few weeks unfolded.

He walked out of his office and there was Louise, walking with a woman in labour. She caught his eye and gave him a wink.

Anton smiled in return.

The tease was back on.

CHAPTER NINE

'I AM SO, so jealous!' Emily said, as Louise teetered in on high heels on Friday night, having finished her shift and got changed into her Christmas party clothes.

'It's fine that you're jealous,' Louise said to Emily, 'because I am so, so jealous of you. I'd love to be in bed now, nursing my bump.'

'You look stunning,' Hugh said.

Louise was dressed in a willow-green dress that clung to her lack of curves and she had her Mistletoe range stockings on, which came with matching panties, bra and suspenders. As they chatted Louise topped her outfit off with a very red coat that looked more like a cape and was a piece of art in itself.

'God help Anton,' Hugh said openly to Louise.

'Sadly, he's stuck on the ward.' Louise rolled her eyes. 'So that was a waste of six pounds.'

As she headed out Hugh turned to Emily, who was trying not to laugh at Hugh's reaction.

'Was she talking about condoms?' Hugh asked.

'She was.'

Oh, Louise was!

As she approached the elevator, there was Anton and his patient must have been sorted because he had changed out of scrubs and was wearing black jeans and a black jumper and looked as festive as one might expect for Anton. He smelt divine, though, Louise thought as she stood beside him, waiting for the lift. 'You've escaped for the weekend,' Louise said.

'I have.'

'Me too!'

She looked at the clothes he was wearing. Black trousers, a black shirt and a very dark grey coat. He looked fantastic rather than festive. 'I didn't know they did out-of-hours funerals,' Louise said as they stepped into the elevator and her eyes ran over his attire.

'You would have me in a reindeer jumper.'

'With a glow stick round your neck,' Louise

said as she selected the ground floor. 'It will be fun tonight.'

'Well, I'm just going to put my head in to be polite,' Anton said. 'I don't want to stay long.'

'Yawn, yawn,' Louise said. 'You really are a misery at Christmas, Anton. Well, I'm staying right to the end. I missed out on far too many parties last year.'

She leant against the wall and gave him a smile when she saw he was looking at her.

'You look very nice,' Anton said.

'Thank you,' Louise responded, and she felt a little rush as his eyes raked over her body and this time Anton did look down, all the way to her toes and then back up to her eyes.

She resented that the lift jolted and that the doors opened and someone came in. They all stood in silence but this was no socially awkward nightmare. His delicious, slow perusal continued all the way to the ground floor.

'Do you want a lift to the party?' Anton offered.

'It's a five-minute walk,' Louise said. 'Come back later for your car.'

They stepped out and it was snowing, just a little. It was too damp and not cold enough for it to settle but there in the light of the streetlamps she could see the flakes floating in the night and he saw her smile and chose to walk the short distance.

It was cold, though, and Louise hated the cold.

'I should have worn a more sensible coat,' Louise said through chattering teeth because her coat, though divine, was a bit flimsy. It was the perfect red, though, and squishy and soft, and she dragged it out every December and she explained that to Anton. 'But this is my Christmas party coat. It wasn't the most thought-out purchase of my life.'

'You have a Christmas coat?'

'I have a Christmas wardrobe,' Louise corrected. 'So, you're just staying for a little while.'

'No,' Anton said.

'Oh, I thought you said—'

'You ruined my line. I was going to suggest

that you leave five minutes after me but then you said that you were looking forward to it.'

'Oh!'

'I think you are right and that we should enjoy Christmas, perhaps together, and stop concerning ourselves with other things.' He stopped walking and so did she and they faced each other in the night and he pulled her into his lovely warm coat. 'Can you be discreet?'

'Not really,' Louise said with a smile, 'but I am discreet about important things.'

'I know.'

'And having a nice Christmas is a very important thing,' she went on, 'so, yes, I'll be discreet.'

Pressed together, her hands under his coat and around his waist there was nothing discreet about Anton's erection.

'I would kiss you but…' He looked down at her perfectly painted lips for about half a second because he didn't care if it ruined her make-up and neither did she. It had been a very long December, all made worth it by this.

After close to two weeks of deprivation Louise returned to his mouth. His kiss was warm and his lips tender. It was a gentle kiss but it delivered such promise. His tongue was hers again to enjoy. His hands moved under her coat and stroked her back and waist so lightly it was almost a tickle, and when their lips parted their faces barely broke contact and Louise's short breaths blew white in the night. She was ridiculously turned on in his arms.

'We need get there,' Anton said.

'Should we arrive together?' Louise asked. 'If we're going to be discreet?'

'Of course,' Anton said, 'we left work at the same time.'

She went into her bag, which was as well organised as her pockets at work, and did a quick repair job on her face and handed Anton a baby wipe.

'Actually, have the packet,' Louise said, and Anton pocketed it with a smile.

He might rather be needing them.

It was everything a Christmas party should be.

The theme was fun and midwives knew how to have it.

All the Christmas music was playing and Louise was the happiest she had been in a very, very long time amongst her colleagues and friends. Anton was there in the background, making her toes curl in her strappy stilettoes as she danced and had fun and made merry with friends while he suitably ignored her. Now and then, though, they caught the other's eye and had a little smile.

It was far less formal than the theatre do and everyone let off a little seasonal steam, well, everyone but Anton.

He stood chatting with Stephanie and Rory, holding his sparkling water, even though he was off duty now until Monday.

'Louise,' Rory called to her near the end of the evening, 'what are you doing for Emily at Christmas?'

'I don't know,' Louise said. 'I've been racking my brains. She's got everything she needs really but I'm going Christmas shopping tomorrow. I might think of something then.'

'Well, let me know if you want to go halves,'

Rory said. 'Or if you see something I could get, then could you get it for me?'

'I shall.'

'I'm going to take Stephanie home,' Rory said, and as Stephanie went to get her coat, even though Anton was there, Louise couldn't resist, once Stephanie had gone, asking Rory a question.

'Is it Stephanie?'

'Who?'

'The woman you like.'

'God.' Rory rolled his eyes. 'Why did I ever say anything?'

'Because we're friends.'

'Just drop it,' Rory said. 'And, no, it's not Stephanie.' He let out a laugh at Louise's suggestion. 'She's married with two children.'

'Maybe that's why you have to keep it so quiet.'

'Louise, it's not Stephanie and you are to leave this alone.' He looked at Anton. 'She's relentless.'

'She is.'

Louise pulled a face at Rory's departing back and then turned and it was just she and Anton.

'Do you want a drink?' Anton asked.

'No, thanks,' Louise said. 'I've had one snowball too many.'

'What *are* you drinking?' Anton asked, because he had seen the pale yellow concoction she had been drinking all night.

'Snowballs—Advocaat, lemonade and lime juice,' she pulled a face.

'You don't like them?'

'I like the *idea* of them,' Louise said, and then her attention was shot as a song came on. 'Ooh, I love this one…'

'Of course you do.'

'No, seriously, it's my favourite.'

It was dance with her or watch her dance alone.

'I thought we were being discreet?' Louise said.

'It's just a dance,' Anton said, as she draped her arms round his neck. 'But Rory's right—you are relentless.'

'I know I am.' Louise smiled.

They were as discreet as two bodies on fire could be, just swaying and looking at each other and talking.

'I want to kiss you under the mistletoe,' Anton said.

'I assume we're not talking about the sad bunch hanging at the bar.'

'No.'

'Did you know these stockings come with matching underwear?'

'I do,' Anton said, 'I saw your work in the magazine.'

'Did you like?'

'I like.' Anton nodded. 'As I said, I want to kiss you under the mistletoe.'

'I am so turned on.' She stated the obvious because he could feel every breath that blew from her lips, he could see her pulse galloping in her neck as well as the arousal in her eyes.

'Good.'

'We need to leave,' Louise said.

'I'm going to go and speak to Brenda and then

leave, and you're going to hang around for a little while and then we meet at my car.'

'I live a two-minute walk from here,' Louise said.

'Okay…'

She loved his slow smile as she gave him her address. 'I'll slip the key into your coat pocket,' Louise said. 'You can go and put the kettle on.'

'I shall.'

'Please don't,' Louise said. 'I meant—'

'Oh, I get what you meant.'

Anton said his goodbyes and chatted with Brenda for an aching ten minutes, though on the periphery of his vision he could see Louise near the coats but then off she went, back to the dance floor.

Anton headed out into the night and found her home very easily. Louise had left the heating on. She loathed coming home to a cold house and a furnace of heat hit Anton as he opened the door as well as the dazzle of decorations, which were about as subtle as Louise.

And as for the bedroom!

Anton couldn't help but smile as he stepped inside Madame Louise's chamber. He looked at the crushed velvet bed that matched the crushed velvet chair by the dressing table and he looked at the array of bottles and make-up on it.

Anton undressed and got into her lovely bed. He had never met someone so unabashed and he liked that about her, liked that she was who she was.

Louise had never been more in demand than in the ten minutes at the end of the party. Everyone, *everyone* wanted her to stop for a chat, and just as she finally got her coat on and was leaving, Brenda suggested they drop over to Louise's as some work dos often ended up there.

'I can't tonight,' Louise said. 'Mum's over.'

'Your mum?'

'I think she and Dad had a row,' Louise lied, but she had to, as her mind danced with a sudden vision of a naked Anton in the hallway greeting half of the maternity staff. 'It's a bit of a sensitive point.'

Louise texted him as she walked out.

I just told the biggest lie

Should I be worried that there is a crib in your bedroom? Anton texted back.

She laughed because she had already told him it was for Emily's baby and it was wrapped in Cellophane too, so she continued the tease.

Aren't we making a baby tonight? Louise fired back.

Get here!!!

She waved as a car carrying her friends tooted, trying not to run on shaky, want-filled legs, and almost breaking her ankle as she walked far too fast for her stilettoes.

She could barely get the key in the door, just so delighted by the turn of events—that they were going to put other things on hold and simply enjoy. Her coat dropped to the floor as she stepped into the bedroom and there he was, naked in her bed and a Christmas wish came true.

'Who's been sleeping in my bed?' Louise smiled.

'No sleeping tonight,' Anton said. 'Come here.'

Louise was not shy; she went straight over, kneeling on her bed and kissing him without restraint.

It was urgent.

Anton was at the tie of her dress as their mouths bruised each other's. He tried to peel it off over arms that were bent because she was holding his head, tonguing him, wanting him, but there was something she first had to do.

'I have to take my make-up off.'

'I'll lick it off.'

'Seriously.' She could hardly breathe, she was somehow straddling him, her dress gaped open and it would be so much easier not to reach for the cold cream. 'It's not vanity, it's work ethic—I'll look like a pizza for my photo shoot otherwise…'

She climbed off the bed and shed her dress and Anton got the full effect of her stunning underwear, and as beautiful as the pictures had been he far preferred the un-airbrushed version.

Louise sat on her chair and slathered her face in cold cream, quickly wiping it off and wishing she hadn't worn so much mascara. Just as she had finished she felt the chair turn and she was face to groin with a naked Anton.

'Poor Anton,' Louise said.

'Not any more,' Anton said, as she started to stroke him. She went to lower her head but he was starting to kneel.

'Stay…' Louise said, because she wanted to taste him.

'You can have it later.'

He caressed the insides of her thighs through her stockings then the white naked flesh so slowly that she was twitching. He stroked her through her damp panties till he moved them aside and explored her again with his fingers till she could almost stand it no more. Her thighs were shaking and finally his hands went for her mistletoe panties and slid them down so slowly that Louise was squirming. Anton pulled her bottom right to the edge of the chair and then took one stockinged leg and put it over his shoulder and then slowly did the same with the other. Such was the greed in his eyes she was almost coming as finally he did kiss what had been under the silken mistletoe.

Louise looked down but his eyes were closed in concentration and her knees started to bend to the skill of his mouth but hands came up and clamped her legs down, so there was nowhere to go but ecstasy.

She felt the cool blowing of his breath and then the warm suction of his mouth and then another soft blow that did nothing to put the fire out. In fact, her hips were lifting, but his mouth would not allow them to.

'Anton…' She didn't need to tell him she was coming, he was lost in it too, moaning, as her thighs clamped his head and she pulsed in his mouth. Anton reached for his cock on instinct. He was close to coming too. He raised himself up, and was stroking himself at her entrance.

They were in the most dangerous of places, two people who definitely should know better.

Louise was frantically patting the dressing table behind her, trying to find a drawer, while watching the silver bead at his tip swelling and drizzling.

'Here…' She pulled out a foil packet and ripped it open. She slid it onto his thick length and there was no way they could make it to the bed, but Anton took a turn in the lucky chair and she leapt on his lap. His mouth sucked her breast through her bra as she wriggled into position.

She hovered provocatively over his erection, revelling for a brief moment in the sensation of his mouth and the anticipation of lowering herself. Anton had worked the fabric down and was now at her nipple, her small breast consumed by his mouth, and then his patience expired. His hands pulled her hips down and in one rapid motion Louise was filled by him, a delicious searing but, better still, his hands did not leave her. Her bedroom was like a sauna and the sheen on her body had her a little slippery but his hands gripped her and did not relent, for she would match his needs.

It had her feeling dizzy—the sensation of being on top while being taken. Louise rested her arms on his shoulders as he pulled her down over and over, and then his mouth lost contact with her breast as he swelled that final time. Her hands went to his head and she ground down, coming with him, squealing in pleasure as they hit a giddy peak. They shared a decadent, wet kiss as he shot inside her, a kiss of possession as she pulsed around his length and her head collapsed onto his shoulder.

Louise kissed his salty shoulder as her breathing finally slowed down.

She could feel him soften inside her and she lifted her head and smiled into his eyes.

'Ready for bed?'

CHAPTER TEN

AFTER ONE HOUR and about seven minutes of sleep they woke to Louise's phone at six.

'I thought you were off today,' Anton groaned.

'I am, but I'm going Christmas shopping.'

'At six a.m.?'

'I want to get a book signed for Mum so I have to line up,' Louise said. 'Stay,' she said, kissing his mouth .'Get up when you're ready, or you can come shopping with me.'

'I'll give it a miss, thanks.'

'Have you done your Christmas shopping?'

'I'll do it online. The shops will be crazy.'

'That's half the fun.' She gave him a nudge. 'Come on.'

She went into the shower and Anton lay there, looking up at the ceiling. He had a couple of things to get. Something for the nurses and his secretary and, yes, he might just as well get it over and done with.

'We'll stop by my place and I can get changed,' Anton said, as she came out of the shower.

'Sure.' Naked, she smiled down at him and lifted her hair. 'Check me for bruises,' she said, while craning her neck and looking down at her buttocks where his fingers had dug in, but, no, they were peachy cream too.

'No need to check,' Anton said, for he had been careful, knowing that she had her photo shoot coming up.

Neither could wait till it was over!

Louise dressed while Anton showered. She pulled on jeans and boots and a massive cream jumper and then she tied up her hair and added a coat.

Anton put on the clothes he had worn last night, though they were stopping by his place so he could get changed.

'Ready to do battle?' she asked, thrilled that Anton had agreed to come along with her. She was determined to Christmas him up, especially when they arrived at his apartment.

'You really are a misery,' Louise said, stepping in. She didn't care about the view or the gorgeous furnishings in his apartment—what she cared about was that there wasn't a single decoration. There were a few Christmas cards stacked with his mail on the kitchen bench but, apart from that, it might just as well have been October, instead of just over a week before Christmas.

'Aren't you even going to get a tree?' Louise asked.

'No.'

'Don't you have Christmas trees in Italy?'

'Some,' Anton said, 'but we go more for nativity scenes and lights.'

'You have to do something.'

'I'm hardly ever here, Louise,' Anton said.

'It's not the point. When you come home—'

'I don't like Christmas,' Anton said, but then amended, 'Although I am starting to really enjoy this one.'

'What do you have to get today?'

'I need to get something for my secretary,' Anton said. 'Perfume?'

'Maybe,' Louise said. 'What sort of things does she like?'

Anton spread out his hands—he really had no idea what Shirley liked.

'What sort of things does she talk about?'

'My diary.'

'God, you're so antisocial,' Louise said.

'Oh, she likes cooking,' Anton recalled. 'She's always bringing in things that she's made.'

'Then I have the perfect present,' Louise said, 'because I'm getting it for my mum. That's what we're going to line up for.'

It wasn't just a book. The first twenty people had the option to purchase a morning's cooking lesson with a celebrity chef. It was fabulous and expensive and with it all going to charity it was well worth it.

Celebrating their success at getting the signed books and cookery lessons, at ten a.m., having

coffee and cake in an already crowded department store, they chatted.

'If your mother can't cook, why would you
spend all that money? Surely it will be wasted?'

'Oh, no.' Louise shook her head. 'If she learns
even one thing and gets it right, my dad will be
grateful for ever—the poor thing,' she added.
'He has to eat it night after night after night. I
usually wriggle out of it when I go and visit. I'll
go over tomorrow and say I've just eaten, but
you can't do that on Christmas Day.'

'How bad is it?'

'It's terrible. I don't know how she does it. It
always looks okay and she thinks it tastes amazing but I swear it's like she's put it in a blender
with water added, burnt it and then put it back
together to look like a dinner again...' She took
out her list. 'Come on, off we go.'

Louise was a brilliant shopper, not that Anton
easily fathomed her methods.

'I adore this colour,' Louise said, trying lipstick on the back of her hand. 'Oh, but this one
is even better.'

'I thought we were here for your sisters.'

'Oh, they're so easy to buy for,' Louise said. 'Anything I love they want to pinch, so anything I love I know they'll like.'

Make-up, perfume, a pair of boots… 'I'm the same size as Chloe,' she explained, as she tried them on. 'It's so good you're here, I'd have had to make two trips otherwise.'

Bag after bag was loaded with gifts. 'I want to go here,' Louise said, and they got off the escalator at the baby section. 'I'm going to get something for Emily and Hugh's baby,' Louise said. 'Hopefully it will be a waste of money and I can give it to NICU.' She looked at Anton. 'Do you think she'll get to Christmas?'

'I hope so,' Anton said. 'I'm aiming for thirty-three weeks.'

Louise heard the unvoiced *but* and for now chose to ignore it.

They went to the premature baby section and found some tiny outfits and there was one perk to being the obstetrician and midwife shopping for a pregnant friend, they knew what colour to get! Louise said yes to gift-wrapping and they waited as it was beautifully wrapped and then topped with a bow.

'I'll keep it in my locker at work,' Louise said.

It was a lovely, lovely, lovely day of shopping, punctuated with kisses. Neither cared about the grumbles they caused as they blocked the pavement or the escalators when they simply had to kiss the other and by the end Louise was seriously, happily worn out.

'You want to get dinner?' Anton offered.

'Take-out?' Louise suggested. 'But we'll have it at my place. I'm not going to your miserable apartment.'

'I have to go back,' Anton said. 'I have to do an hour's work at least.'

'Fine,' Louise conceded, 'but we'll drop these back at my place first and I'll get some clothes.'

'You won't need them,' Anton said, but Louise was insistent.

All her presents she put in the bedroom. 'I can't wait to wrap them,' Louise said. 'I'll just grab a change of clothes and things, you go and make a drink.'

Louise grabbed more than a change of clothes. In fact, she went into her wardrobe and pulled out some leftover Christmas decorations and stuffed them all into a not so small overnight bag. She also took the tiny silver tree that she'd been meaning to put up at the nurses' station but kept forgetting to take.

'How long are you staying for?' Anton asked, when she came out and he saw the size of her overnight bag.

'Till you kick me out.' Louise gave him a kiss. 'I like to be prepared.'

Anton really did have work to do.

A couple of blood tests were in and he went through them, and there was a patient at thirteen weeks' gestation who was bleeding. Anton went into his study and rang her to check how things were.

Louise could hear him safely talking and quickly set to work.

The little tree she put on his coffee table and

she draped some tinsel on the window ledges and put up some stars, a touch worried she might leave some marks on his walls but he'd just have to get over it, Louise decided.

She took out her can and sprayed snow on his gleaming windows, and oh, it looked lovely.

'What the hell have you done?' Anton said, as he came into the lounge, but he was smiling.

'I need nice things around me,' Louise said, 'happy things.'

'It would seem,' Anton said, looking not at her handiwork now but the woman in his arms, 'that so do I.'

CHAPTER ELEVEN

'WHAT HAPPENED LAST Christmas?' Anton asked, late, late on Sunday night. They'd started on the sofa and had watched half a movie and now they lay naked on the floor bathed by the light from the television. 'You said it was tinsel-starved.'

She really would prefer not to talk about it. They had had such a lovely weekend but there were so many parts of so many conversations that they were avoiding, like IVF and Anton's loathing of Christmas, that when he finally broached one of them, Louise answered carefully. There was no way she could tell him all but she told him some.

'I broke up with my boyfriend on Christmas Eve.'

'You said it was tinsel-starved before then, that you didn't go to many parties.'

'It wasn't worth it.'

'In what way?'

'I know you think I'm a flirt…'

'I like that about you.'

'But I'm only really like that with you,' Louise said. 'I mean that. I used to be a shocking flirt and then when I started going out with Wesley… well, I got told off a lot.'

'For flirting with other men?'

'No!' Louise said, shuddering at the memory. 'He decided that if I flirted like that with him, then what was I like when he wasn't there? I don't want to go into it all, but I changed and I hate myself for it. I changed into this one eighth of a person and somehow I got out—on Christmas Eve last year. It took months, just months to even start feeling like myself again.'

'Okay.'

'Do you know the day I did?' Louise asked, smiling as she turned to face him.

'No.'

'We were going to Emily's leaving do and I

saw you in the corridor and I asked you to come along…'

'You were wearing red,' Anton easily recalled. 'You were with Emily.'

'That's right, it was for her leaving do. Well, even when I asked if you wanted to come along, I deep down knew that you wouldn't. I was just…' She couldn't really explain. 'I was just flirting again…sort of safe in the knowledge that it wouldn't go anywhere.'

'But it has,' Anton said.

'I guess.' Louise smiled. 'Have you ever been married?' Louise asked.

'Why do you ask?'

'I just wondered.'

'No,' Anton said. 'Have you?'

'God, no,' Louise said.

'Have you ever come close?'

'No,' Louise admitted.

'You and Rory?'

Louise laughed and shook her head. 'We were only together a few weeks. Just when we started going out I found that it was likely that I was going to have issues getting pregnant. It was terrible timing because it was all I could think about. Poor Rory, he started going out with a happy person and when the doctor broke the news I just plunged into despair. It wasn't his baby I wanted, just the thought I might never have one. It was just all too much for him...' She looked at Anton. 'I think I was just low at that time and that's why I must have taken my bastard alert glasses off. I've made a few poor choices with men since then.' She closed her eyes. 'None worse than Wesley, though.'

'How bad did it get?' Anton asked, but Louise couldn't go there and she shook her head.

'What about you?' Louise asked. 'Have you been serious with anyone?'

'Not really, well, there was one who came close...' It was Anton who stopped talking then.

Anton who shook his head.

He simply couldn't go there with someone who might just want him for a matter of weeks.

CHAPTER TWELVE

'CAN YOU KEEP a close eye on Felicity in seven?' Anton asked. 'She's upset because her husband has been unable to get a flight back till later this evening.'

Felicity was one of Anton's high-risk pregnancies and finally the day had arrived where she would meet her baby, but her husband was in Germany with work.

'How is she doing?' Louise asked.

'Very slowly,' Anton said. 'Hopefully he'll get here in time.' He picked up a parcel, beautifully wrapped by Louise. 'I'm going to give this to Shirley now. She's only in this morning to sort out my diary before she takes three weeks off. Then I will be in the antenatal clinic. Call me if you have any concerns.'

'Yes, Anton,' Louise sighed.

Anton heard her sigh but it did not bother him.

Things were not going to change at work. In fact, he was more overbearing if anything, just because he didn't want a mistake to come between them.

'This is for you,' Anton said, as he went into Shirley's office. 'I just wanted to thank you for all your hard work this year and to say merry Christmas.'

'Thank you, Anton.' Shirley smiled.

'I hope you have a lovely break.'

He went to go, even as she opened it, but her cry of surprise had him turn around.

'How?'

Anton stared. His usually calm secretary was shaking as she spoke.

'How did you manage to get this—there were only twenty places.'

'I got there early.'

'You lined up to get me this! Oh, my...'

Anton felt a little guilt at her obvious delight. It really had been far from a hardship to be huddled in a queue with Louise, but it was Shirley's utter shock too that caused more than a little disquiet.

'I never thought…' Shirley started and then stopped. She could hardly say she'd been expecting some bland present from her miserable boss. 'It's wonderful,' she said instead.

God, Anton thought, was he that bad that a simple nice gesture could reduce a staff member to tears?

Yes.

He nodded to Helen, the antenatal nurse who would be working alongside him, and he saw that she gave a slightly strained one back.

Things had to change, Anton realised.

He had to learn to let go a little.

But how?

'How are things?' Louise asked, as she walked into Felicity's room with the CTG machine.

'They're just uncomfortable,' Felicity said. She was determined to have a natural birth and had refused an epidural or anything for pain. 'I'm going to try and have a sleep.'

'Do,' Louise said. 'Do you want me to close the curtains?'

Felicity nodded.

Brenda popped her head in the door. 'Are you going to lunch, Louise?'

'In a minute,' Louise said. 'I'm just doing some obs.' Both Felicity and the baby seemed fine. 'I'll leave this on while I have my lunch,' Louise said about the CTG machine, and Felicity nodded. 'Then later we might have a little walk around, but for now just try and get some rest.'

She closed the curtains and moved a blanket over Felicity, who was half-asleep, and left her to the sound of her baby's heartbeat. Louise would check the tracing when she came back from her break and see the pattern of the contractions.

'Press the bell if you need anything and I'll be here.'

'But you're going to lunch.'

'Yep, but that buzzer is set for me, so just you press it if you need to.'

'Thanks, Louise,' Felicity said. 'What time are you here till?'

Louise thought before answering. 'I'm not sure.'

Louise left the door just a little open so that her colleagues could easily pop in and out and could hear the CTG, then headed to the fridge and got out her lunch.

'Fancy company?' Louise asked Emily as she knocked on her open door.

'Oh, yes!' Emily sat up in the bed. 'How was the party?'

'Excellent.'

'Why didn't you text me all weekend?'

'I did!' Louise said.

'Five-thirty on a Sunday evening suggests to me you were otherwise engaged.'

'I was busy,' Louise said, 'Christmas shopping!'

'You lie,' Emily said.

'Actually, I need to charge my phone,' Louise said, because she hadn't been back home since being at Anton's. 'Can I borrow your charger?'

'Sure.' Emily smiled. 'That's not like you.'

Louise said nothing. She certainly wasn't

going to admit to Emily her three-night fest with Anton. As she plugged in her phone and sat down, the background noise of Felicity's baby's heartbeat slowed. Louise was so tuned into that noise, as all midwives were, and she didn't like what she had just heard.

'Are you okay?' Emily asked.

'I think I've got restless leg syndrome.' Louise gave a light response. 'I'm just going to check on someone and then I'll be back.'

She went quietly into Felicity's room. Felicity was dozing and Louise warmed her hand and then slipped it on Felicity's stomach, watching the monitor and patiently waiting for a contraction to come.

'It's just me,' Louise whispered, as Felicity woke up as a contraction deepened and Emily watched as the baby's heart rate dipped. She checked Felicity's pulse to make sure the slower heart rate that the monitor was picking up wasn't Felicity's.

'Turn onto your other side for me,' Louise said to the sleepy woman, and helped Felicity to get on her left side and looked up as Brenda, alerted by the sound of the dip in the baby's heart rate, looked in.

'Page Anton,' Louise said.

Even on her left side the baby's heart rate was dipping during contractions and Louise put some oxygen on Felicity. 'We'll move her over to Delivery,' Brenda said.

'Have you heard from Anton?'

'I've paged him but he hasn't answered,' Brenda said.

'I'll see if he's in the staffroom.'

Louise raced around to check but Anton wasn't there.

She paged him again and then they moved Felicity through to the delivery ward. They were about to move her onto the delivery bed but Louise decided to wait for Anton before doing that as she listened to the baby's heart rate. The way this baby was behaving, they might be running to Theatre any time soon.

She typed in an urgent page for Anton but when there was still no response Louise remembered her phone was in Emily's room. 'Text him,' Louise said to Brenda, and, ripping off a tracing, Louise left Felicity with Brenda and swiftly went to a phone out of earshot.

'Are the pagers working?' she asked the switchboard operator. 'I need Anton Rossi paged and, in case he's busy, I need the second on paged too, urgently.'

She then rang Theatre and, because she had worked there for more than five years, when she rang and explained they might need a theatre very soon, she knew she was being taken seriously and that they would immediately be setting up for a Caesarean.

'I can't get hold of Anton,' Louise said, but then she saw him, his phone in hand, racing towards them. 'Anton! Felicity's having late decelerations. Foetal heart rate is dropping to sixty.'

'How long has this been going on?'

'About fifteen minutes.'

'And you didn't think to tell me sooner! Hell! If Brenda hadn't texted me…' Anton hissed, taking the tracing and looking at it in horror, because time was of the essence. With pretty much one look at the tracing the decision to operate was made. For Anton it was a done deal.

It was like some horrific replay of what had happened two years ago.

'I paged you when it first happened,' Louise said, but there wasn't time for explanations now. As Anton went into the delivery room the overhead speakers crackled into life.

'System error. Professor Hadfield, can you make your way straight to Emergency? Mr Rossi, Delivery Ward, room two.'

Anton briefly closed his eyes.

'Mr Rossi, urgently make your way to Delivery, room two. System error—pagers are down.'

And so it repeated.

'Is that for me?' Felicity cried, terrified by the urgency of the calls overhead.

'Hey…' Louise gave Felicity a cuddle as Anton examined her. 'It's just that the pagers are down and so I had to use my whip a bit on Switchboard to get Anton here.'

'Felicity.' Anton came up to the head-end of

the bed. 'Your baby is struggling...' Everything had been done. She was on her side, oxygen was on and she was still on the bed so they could simply speed her to Theatre. 'We're going to take you to Theatre now and do a Caesarean section.'

'Can I be awake at least?'

'We really do need to get your baby out now.'

'I'll be there with you,' Louise said, as the porter arrived. 'I am not leaving your side, I promise you. I can take some pictures of your baby if you like,' Louise offered, and Felicity gave her her phone.

'Can you let Theatre know?' Anton said, before he raced ahead to scrub.

It took everything she could muster to keep the bitterness from her voice. 'I already have, Anton.'

Louise and the porter whisked the bed down the corridor. There was no consent form to be signed—that had been taken care of at the antenatal stage.

'I'm so scared,' Felicity said, as they wheeled her into Theatre.

'I know,' Louise said, cleaning down her shoes and popping on shoe covers, then she put on a theatre hat and gown. 'You've got the best obstetrician,' Louise said. 'I've seen him do many Caesareans and he's brilliant.'

'I know.'

The bed was wheeled through and Louise's old colleagues were waiting. Connor and Miriam helped Louise to get Felicity onto the theatre table and she smiled when she saw Rory arrive. He was a bit breathless and as he caught his breath Louise spoke on. 'You've got an amazing anaesthetist too. Hi, Rory, this is Felicity.'

Rory was lovely with Felicity and went through any allergies and previous anaesthetics and things. 'I'm going to be by your side every minute,' he said to Felicity. 'Till you're awake again, here is where I'll be.'

'I'll be here too,' Louise said.

Theatre was filling. The paediatric team was

arriving as Rory slipped the first drug into Felicity's IV.

'Think baby thoughts,' Louise said with a smile as Felicity went under.

Louise was completely supernumerary at this point. She was simply here on love watch for one of her mums. And so, once Felicity had been intubated, Louise simply closed her mind to everything, even bastard Anton. She just sat on a stool and thought lovely baby thoughts.

She heard the swirl of suction and a few curses from Anton as he tried to get one very flat baby out as quickly as possible.

Then there was silence and she looked up as a rather floppy baby was whisked away and she kept thinking baby thoughts as they rubbed it very vigorously and flicked at its little feet. She glanced at Rory as another anaesthetist started to bag him.

But then Rory smiled and Louise looked round and watched as the baby shuddered and she watched as his little legs started to kick and his hands started to fight. His cries of protest were muffled by the oxygen mask but were the most beautiful sounds in the world.

Louise didn't look at Anton, she just told Felicity that her baby was beautiful, wonderful, that he was crying and could she hear him, even though Felicity was still under anaesthetic.

Anton did look at Louise.

She did that, Anton thought.

She made all his patients relax and laugh, and though Felicity could not know what was being said, still Louise said it.

He could have honestly kicked himself for his reaction but, God, it had been almost a replica of what had happened back in Italy.

'He's beautiful,' Louise said over and over.

So too was Louise, Anton thought, knowing he'd just blown any chance for them.

Louise *was* beautiful, even when she was raging.

Not an hour later she marched into the male changing room and slammed the door shut.

'Hey, Louise,' called Rory, who was just getting changed. 'You're in the wrong room.'

'Oh, I'm in the right room,' Louise said. 'Could you excuse us, Rory, please?'

'We will do this in my office,' Anton said. Wet from the shower, a towel around his loins, he did not want to do this now, but Louise had no intention of waiting till he got dressed. She was far, far beyond furious.

'Oh, no, this won't keep.'

'Good luck,' Rory called to Anton as he left them to it.

And then it was just Louise and Anton but even as he went to apologise for what had happened earlier, or to even explain, Louise got in first.

'You can question my morals, you can think what you like about me, but don't you ever, ever—'

'Question your morals?' Anton checked. 'Where the hell did that come from?'

'Don't interrupt me,' Louise raged. 'I've had it with you. What you accused me of today—'

'Louise.'

'No!' She would not hear it.

'I apologise. I did not realise the pagers were down.'

'I did,' Louise said instantly. 'When you didn't come, or make contact, it was the first thing I thought—not that you were negligent and simply couldn't be bothered to get here...'

Her lips were white she was so angry. 'I'm going to speak to Brenda and put in an incident report about the pagers today, and while I'm there I'm going to tell her I don't want to work with you any more.'

'That's a bit extreme.'

'It's isn't extreme. I've thought about doing it before.' She saw him blink in surprise. 'Everything I do you check again—'

'Louise...' Anton wasn't about to deny it. He checked on her more than the other midwives, he was aware of that. In trying to protect her, to protect *them*, from what had happened to him and Dahnya, he had gone over the top. 'If I can explain—'

But Louise was beyond hearing him. She lost her temper then and Louise hadn't lost her temper since that terrible day. 'You don't want a midwife,' Louise shouted, 'you want a doula, rubbing the mums' backs and offering support. Well, I'm over it, Anton. Have you any idea how demoralising it is?' she raged, though possibly she was talking more to Wesley than Anton. 'Have you any idea how humiliating it is…?'

Anton took a step forward, to speak, to calm her down, and then stood frozen as he heard the fear in her voice.

'Get off me!' She put her hands up in defence and there was a shocked moment of silence when she realised what she had said, what she had done, but then came his calm voice.

'I'm not touching you, Louise.'

She pressed her hands to her face and her fingers to her eyes. 'I'm sorry,' Louise said, 'not for what I said before but—'

'It's okay.' Anton was breathless too, as if her unleashed fear had somehow attached to him. 'We'll talk when you've calmed down.'

'No.' Louise shook her head, embarrassed at

her outburst but still cross. 'We won't talk because I don't want to hear it, Anton.' And then turned and left.

She was done.

CHAPTER THIRTEEN

'WHAT HAPPENED?' EMILY asked, when Louise returned a couple of hours later to the ward.

'Sorry, I just got waylaid.'

'Louise?'

'I'm fine.'

'You've been crying.'

'There's nothing wrong.'

'Louise?' Emily frowned when she saw Louise's smile was wavering as she took Emily's blood pressure. 'What's going on? Look, I'm bored out of my mind. I mean, I am so seriously bored and I'm fed up with people thinking I can't have a normal conversation, or that they only tell me nice things.' Emily was truly concerned because she hadn't seen red eyes on Louise in a very long time. 'Wesley isn't contacting you again?'

'No, no.' Louise sat down on the bed, even though Brenda might tell her off.

'Tell me.' Emily took her hand.

'Anton.' Louise gulped. Certainly she wasn't going to scare Emily and tell her all that had gone on with Felicity's baby but they really were speaking as friends.

'Okay.'

'Personal or professional?'

'Both,' Louise admitted. 'He checks and double-checks everything, you know what he's like…'

'I do,' Emily said.

'It's like he doesn't trust any of the staff but he does it more with me.'

'Louise.' Emily didn't know whether she should say anything but it was pretty much common knowledge what had happened a few months ago. 'Remember when Gina had her meltdown and went into rehab?'

'Yep, I know, Hugh reported her…' Louise looked at Emily, remembering that there had been more than one complaint, or so the rumours went. 'Did Anton report her as well?'

'I'm saying nothing.'

'Okay.' Louise squeezed her hand in gratitude as Emily spoke on.

'So maybe he feels he has reason to be checking things.'

'Hugh doesn't, though,' Louise pointed out. 'Hugh isn't constantly looking over the nursing staff's shoulders and assuming the worst.'

'I know.' Emily sighed. She adored Anton but had noticed that he was dismissive of the nurses' findings and she could well understand that things might have come to a head. 'So, what's the personal stuff?'

'Do you really need to know that your obstetrician got off with your midwife?'

'Ooh.' Emily gave a delighted smile. 'I think I did really need to know that.'

'Well, it won't be happening again,' Louise said. 'We just had the most terrible row, or rather I did...'

'And what did Anton do?' Emily gently enquired.

'He apologised,' Louise said, and then she frowned because she wasn't very used to a guy backing down. For too long it had been the other way around. 'Emily…' Louise's eyes filled with tears. 'I shouted for him to get off me and the poor guy was just standing there.'

'Oh, Louise…' Emily rubbed Louise's shoulder. 'It must have been terrifying for you to have a big row. Rows are normal, though. What happened to you wasn't.'

'I know.' Louise blew her nose and recovered herself and gave Emily a smile. 'I really let rip.' Louise let out a small shocked laugh.

'She really did!' Anton was at the door and came over to the bed. 'Your latest ultrasound is back. All looks well, there is a nice amount of fluid.' He had a feel of Emily's stomach.

'Nice size,' Anton said.

'Really?'

'Really.' Anton nodded. 'Now is the time they start to plump up and your baby certainly is.'

They headed out of Emily's room and he turned to Louise. 'What is her blood pressure?'

'Ha-ha,' Louise said. 'Check it yourself.'

Anton gave a wry smile as Louise flounced off but it faded when he saw she went straight up to Brenda.

Louise hadn't been lying when she had said she didn't know when she'd be going home.

Something, something had told her she'd be around for the delivery, which meant she wanted to be around when Felicity was more properly awake, and at four she sat holding a big fat baby who had given everyone a horrible scare.

'Your husband just called and he's at Heathrow and is on his way,' Louise said. 'And your mum is on her way too.' Felicity smiled. 'And you have the cutest, most gorgeous baby. In fact, he's so cute I don't think I can hand him over...'

Felicity smiled as Louise did just that and placed the baby in her arms.

'He's gorgeous.'

'I was so scared.'

'I know you were but, honestly, he gave us a fright but he's fine.' She stared at the baby, who was gnawing at his wrist. 'He's beautiful and he's also starving,' Louise said.

'Can I feed him?'

'You can,' Louise said, 'because he's trying to find mine and I've told him I've got nothing…' She looked up as Anton came in and then got back to work, helping a very hungry baby latch on.

'Louise, can I have a word before you leave?' Anton asked.

Louise's response was a casual 'Sure', but Anton knew that was for the sake of the patient.

'Felicity,' Anton said. 'Your mother has just arrived…'

'Do you want me to tell her to wait while you feed?' Louise checked, but Felicity shook her head.

'No, let her in.'

Louise stayed for the first feed. She just loved that part and then when finally the baby was fed and content and in his little isolette she gave

Felicity a cuddle. 'I'll come by tomorrow and we'll talk more about what happened today, if you want to. I took some photos with your phone, if you want to have a look through them with me.'

'Thank you.'

She popped in to see Emily on her way out, as she always did, but she was just about all smiled out. She just wanted to go home for a good cry, a glass of wine and then bed.

She didn't even pretend to smile when she knocked on Anton's office door and went in.

'Can we talk?'

Louise shook her head. 'I don't want to talk to you, Anton,' Louise said. 'I'm tired. I just want to go home.'

'Louise, what happened today was not about you. I had an incident in Milan…'

'I don't want to hear it, Anton,' Louise said, and then relented. 'Imelda's, then,' Louise said. 'I'm just going to get changed.'

'Sure.'

'I'll meet you over there.'

* * *

There was Anton with his sparkling water but
there was a glass of wine and some nachos waiting for Louise. Really, she shouldn't because she
had the bloody photo shoot in less than a week
but Louise shovelled them in her mouth, getting
hungrier with each mouthful.

'Do you want to get something else?'

'These are fine,' Louise said, and then looked
at him. 'Well?'

'I am so very sorry for today. You did everything right, from ringing Theatre to keeping her
on the bed. She was very lucky to have you on
duty and I apologise for jumping to the worst
conclusion.'

Louise gave a tight shrug. It wasn't just today
she was upset about. 'What about the other
days?' she challenged. 'I don't think you trust
me.'

'No.' Anton shook his head. 'That is not the
case.'

'It's very much the case,' Louise said. 'Everything I do you double-check, or you simply

dismiss my findings… Aside from the repeated wallops to my ego, it's surely doubling up for the patient.' Louise let out a breath. 'So what happened in Milan?'

'A few years ago, on Christmas morning, I took a handover, and I was told everything was fine, but by lunchtime I had a baby dead—' Louise was about to say something but Anton spoke over her. 'It *was* the hospital's fault,' Anton said. 'Apparently the night midwife had told a junior doctor she had concerns; I took the handover from the registrar and those concerns hadn't been passed on to her. It was just complete miscommunication. I went in to see my patient at ten, and there were many things that I should have been paged about but hadn't been. I took her straight to Theatre and delivered the baby but he only lived for a couple of hours.

'The coroner did not blame me, thank God, but I have never seen friendships fall so rapidly. There was blame, accusations, it was hell. So much so that when the finding came in I no longer trusted anyone I worked with, and I knew

I had to make a fresh start, which was why I moved into fertility.'

'But you came back.'

'Yes, I never thought I would but the last months I was there, the parents of Alberto, the baby who had died, came in to try for another baby. It was a shock to us all. I offered to step aside but by then I had quite a good reputation and they asked that I remain. I was very happy when they got pregnant and it was then that I realised how much I had missed obstetrics. I knew I needed a fresh start so I applied to come here. I had always had a good rapport with colleagues until Alberto's death. I wanted to get that back and I tried, but within a few weeks of being here there was an incident...' He looked at Louise and she was glad that Emily had filled her in about Gina because Anton didn't. 'I'm not giving specifics but it shook me and from that point I have been cautious...'

'To the extreme,' Louise said.

'Yes.'

'Terrible things happen, Anton. Terrible, terrible things…'

'I know that. I just wish I had not taken a handover that morning and had checked myself…'

'You can't check everyone, you can't follow everyone around.'

'I'm aware of that.'

'Yet you do.'

'I've spoken to Brenda and I have told her what went on, not just today but in the past. I also told her that I am hoping things will be different in the future.'

'Did you get her "There's no I in team" lecture?' Louise asked, and Anton smiled and nodded.

'I've had it a few times from Brenda already and, yes, I got it again today.'

'Well, I disagree with her,' Louise said. 'There should be an I in team. I am responsible, I am capable, I know I've got this, and if I stuff up then I take responsibility. If we all do that, which we seem to do where I work, then teams do well. We look out for each other,' Louise said. 'We have a buddy system. I don't just glance at CTGs when they're given to me and neither do my colleagues. We take ages discussing them, going over them…'

'I know that.'

'It doesn't feel like it,' Louise said.

'I am hoping things will be different now.'

'Good,' Louise said. 'Is that it?'

'No, I want to know what you meant about me judging you on your morals.'

'This isn't a social get-together, Anton. I'm here to talk about work.'

'Louise.'

'Okay, just because I'm not on a husband hunt, just because I fancied you…'

'Past tense?'

'Oh, it is so past tense,' Louise said. 'So very past tense.'

'Louise,' Anton said, and she must have heard the tentative tone to his voice because immediately her eyes darted away, even before his question was voiced. 'What happened that made you so scared back there?'

'That isn't about work either.' She got up and hoisted up her bag. 'I'm sorry you went through crap and I'm so sorry for the baby and its family.'

'Louise.' He halted her as she went to go. 'The midwife on that morning, I was going out with her. She was busy, meant to go back and check, meant to call, but got waylaid. Can you see why I was very reluctant to get involved with you?'

'I can.' She stood there but didn't give him the answer he was hoping for. 'Well, at least you don't have that problem with me now—we're no longer involved.' She gave him a tight smile. 'Goodnight, Anton.'

Louise got home, closed the door and promptly burst into tears. Despite her tough talk with Anton she could think of nothing worse than losing a baby under those circumstances and at Christmas too.

Then she went into the bath and cried some

more. She'd been raging at him and he'd simply stood there.

She was beyond confused and all churned up from her loss of control.

Why couldn't it just be sex? Louise thought. Why did she have to really, really like him?

As she got out of the bath her phone bleeped a text from Emily.

U OK?

Louise gave a rapid reply.

Bloody men! How's baby?

Kick-kicking, or maybe he's waving to you.

Louise sent back a smiley face, knowing what was to come.

Maybe SHE'S waving???? Emily texted, hoping that Louise would give her a clue.

Not telling, came Louise's reply. Ask Hugh.

He won't tell me, Emily replied. Bloody men!

CHAPTER FOURTEEN

ANTON REALLY DID make an effort at work, though Louise wasn't sure if it was temporary. At least he had stopped double-checking everything that she did. Brenda had a word with some of the staff, as Anton had asked her to do. They in turn rang him a little sooner than usual with concerns, and slowly the I in team was working, except Louise was no longer a part of his team.

'Phone for you, Louise,' someone called, and Louise headed out to the desk. It was the IVF clinic, which had been unable to reach her on her mobile or at home, and Louise took out her phone and saw that the battery was flat.

'Are you okay to talk, or do you want to call us back?'

'No, now's fine,' Louise said.

'Richard wanted to let you know that your

iron levels are now normal but to keep taking the supplements, especially the folic acid.'

'I shall. Thank you,' Louise said.

'Have a lovely Christmas and we'll see you in the new year.'

Louise's stomach was all aflutter as she ended the call.

'Good news?' Brenda asked, but Louise didn't answer. Her *lovely Christmas* was walking past and this time when he sat down and ignored her it was at Louise's request.

Of course, she still dealt with his patients— after all, Emily was one of them—but the distance she had asked for was there. As far as was reasonable she was allocated other patients and when they spoke it was only about work.

'Can you buddy this?' Beth asked, and Louise nodded and sat down. 'What are you working over Christmas?' Beth asked.

'Tomorrow's my last shift,' Louise said, 'and then I'm off till after New Year.'

'Lucky you!'

'I know.' Louise smiled. 'I can't wait.'

She lied.

They looked at the CTG together and Anton could hear them discussing it, Louise asking a couple of questions before they both signed off on it.

What a mistrusting fool he had been.

He had never worked anywhere better than here. The diligence, the care, was second to none but he'd realised it all too late.

'Do you need anything, Anton?' Beth asked, as Anton signed off on a few prescriptions and then stood.

'Nope, I'm heading home. Goodnight, everyone.'

When Anton stepped into his apartment a little later he felt like ripping the bloody tinsel down, yet he left it.

Louise had been in his apartment for three nights in total yet she was everywhere.

From lipstick on the towels and sheets to long blonde hairs in his comb.

Even the bed smelt of her perfume and Anton woke to his phone buzzing at three-thirty a.m.

and, for a second, so consuming was her scent he actually thought she was in bed beside him.

Instead, it was the ward with news about Emily.

'I'm so sorry…' Emily said, as Anton came into the room at four a.m.

'No apologies,' Anton said, taking off his jacket, and then smiled at Evie, who had set up for Anton to examine Emily.

'I thought I'd wet myself,' Emily said. 'Maybe I did…'

'It is amniotic fluid,' Anton said, taking a swab. 'Your waters are leaking. We will get this swab checked for any signs of infection and keep a close eye on your temperature.'

'How long can I go with a leak?'

'Variable. Do you have any discomfort?'

'My back aches,' Emily said, 'but I'm not sure if that's from being in bed…'

'Have you told Hugh?'

'Not yet,' Emily said. 'He was paged at midnight and he's in Theatre. He'll find out soon enough.'

* * *

When Louise came on for her shift she saw Anton sitting at the desk and duly ignored him. She headed around to the kitchen and made herself a cup of tea, trying to ignore the scent and feel of him when he walked into the kitchen behind her.

'Emily's waters are leaking,' Anton said. 'I just thought I'd tell you now, rather than you hear it during handover.'

Louise turned round.

'I've ordered an ultrasound to check the amniotic levels and she is on antibiotics…'

'But?'

'Her back is hurting again. There are no contractions but her uterus is irritable.'

'She's going to have it.'

'You don't know that's the case…'

'I do know that this baby is coming soon,' Louise said, and Anton nodded.

'I don't think she'll hold off for much longer.'

Louise felt her eyes fill up when Anton spoke on.

'I miss working with you, Louise.'

Louise didn't say anything.

'I miss *you*,' Anton said.

She looked at him and, yes, she missed him too.

'Can we start again?' Anton said.

'I don't know.'

'Louise, you seem to have it in your head that I'm controlling. I get that I have been at work, I still will be...' He looked at her. 'Do you know why I've been on water at all the parties over Christmas? It's because I have Hazel who is due to deliver soon and I believe Emily will have that baby any day. I want to be there for them both. Yes, I am fully in control at work, and I get you have seen me at my worst here, but you know why now.'

Louise breathed out and looked at him, the most diligent person she knew, and then he continued speaking.

'You explained you are dieting because you have a photo shoot, that you know what you're doing with your weight, and not once since then have I said anything. I was worried about you because my sister has been there but when you said you knew what you were doing, I accepted that.'

He had.

'My ex…' she didn't want to say it here but it was time to tell him a little, if not all. 'He was so jealous, he didn't get that I could be friends with Rory. He didn't even like Emily…'

'And…?' Anton pushed, but Louise shook her head so he pushed on as best he could, but he was a non-witness after the fact and Louise kept him so.

'I would never come between you and your friends.'

'You weren't exactly friendly towards Rory on the night of the theatre do—you were giving him filthy looks.'

'Oh, that's right,' Anton said. 'And you were so sweet to *Saffron*. I was jealous when I thought you were on together, just as you were with me.'

Louise swallowed, she knew he was right.

'I like your friends. I like it that you can be friendly with an ex. And you can flirt, you can be funny, and I have no issue with it, but what I will not do is go along with the notion that I like you going for IVF so early in our relationship.'

Louise turned to go.

'Wrong word for you, Louise?'

It was.

'I need to think, Anton,' Louise said, and possibly the nicest thing he did then was not to argue his case or demand that they speak. He simply nodded.

'Of course.'

Louise took handover and she was allocated Stephanie's patients, all except for Emily, who was asleep when she went in to her.

'Just rest,' Louise said. 'I'm only doing your blood pressure.'

'When are you going for lunch?' Emily asked sleepily.

'About twelve. Do you want me to have it here with you?'

Emily nodded. 'Unless you need a break from the patients.'

'Don't be daft—of course I'd love to have lunch with you.'

When lunchtime came Louise went and got her salad from the fridge and it was so nice to close the door and sit down with her friend.

'It's going to be strange, not having you around,' Emily admitted.

'I'll be visiting, texting…'

'I know,' Emily said, 'it just won't be the same. Are you excited about your photo shoot tomorrow?'

'I am, though you're to promise you'll text me if anything happens.' Louise went into her pocket and handed Emily a business card. 'This is the hotel I'm at, just in case there's nowhere to put my phone!'

'Louise, you are not leaving your photo shoot,' Emily said, handing her back the card.

'But I want to be here if anything happens.'

'I know you do and I'd love you to be here, but I've got Hugh.'

Louise took back the card and stared at it.

Emily had Hugh.

Yes, Louise could do this alone and she would, but for a moment there she reconsidered. Hugh had been here every day, making Emily laugh, letting her relax, an endless stream of support.

It would be so hard to do this alone.

Louise cleared her throat. She didn't like where her mind was heading. 'Well, if you can hold off tomorrow, Christmas Day would be fine.' Louise gave her friend a wide smile as she teased her. 'At least that would get me out of dinner at Mum's.'

Emily laughed,

'Have you seen what you're wearing for the photo shoot?' Emily asked.

'Oh, it's so nice, all reds and black—Valentine's Day stuff, seriously sexy,' Louise said. 'We've got the presidential suite and I think I'm his girlfriend or wife, the model's Jeremy...' Louise rattled on as, unseen, Anton came in and checked Emily's CTG. 'He's so gorgeous but so gay. Anyway, we wake up and why I'm wearing a bra and panties and shoes at six a.m. I have no idea, but then there are to be photos with me waving him off to work...'

'Still in your undies and shoes?' Emily asked, and Louise nodded.

'Then he comes home with flowers and I'm in my evening stuff then, and I think he takes me over the dining table…'

Emily wished Louise would turn around and see Anton's smile as she spoke.

'Everything is looking good,' Anton said, and Emily watched as Louise jumped, wondering how much he had heard. Emily's heart actually hurt that Louise expected to be told off for being herself, and she watched her friend make herself turn around and smile.

'Hiya,' Louise said. 'I'm just asking Emily to cross her legs tomorrow, but any time after that is fine.'

'How Emily's temperature?'

'All normal. I'm actually on my lunch break.'

'Oh,' Anton said, and left them to it. 'Sorry for interrupting.'

'Why won't you give the two of you a chance?' Emily said. 'Why can't you believe—?'

'Because I stopped believing,' Louise said.

'I want to believe—I want to believe that we might be able to work, that we're as right for each other, as I sometimes feel we are. I just don't know how to start.'

'Have you told him what happened last Christmas?'

'I don't know how to.'

'He needs to know, Louise. If you two are to stand a chance then you have to somehow tell him.'

Louise shook her head. 'I don't want to talk about it ever again.'

'Why don't you ask Anton to come along tomorrow?'

'Good God, no!'

'Think about it—you at your tarty best. What would Wesley have done?'

'I shudder to think,' Louise said. 'Look, I know Anton's not like that. I'm just so scared because I'd have sworn Wesley wasn't like that either.'

'Well, there's one very easy way to find out.'

'I think he's working tomorrow,' Louise said. 'Anyway, don't you want him here?'

'Oh, believe me, if I go into labour I'll be calling him, so you'd know anyway, but please don't leave your photo shoot for me. I know how important it is to you.'

'Okay,' Louise said. 'I still want to know, though.'

'Ask Anton.'

Louise shook her head. 'He's not going to take a day off for that.'

'He's not going to if you don't ask him.'

Louise checked on a patient who was sleeping but in labour and she put her on the CTG machine and took a footstool and climbed up onto the nurses' station where she sat, watching her patient from a distance, listening to the baby's heartbeat.

Anton walked onto the unit and saw Louise sitting up on the bench, back straight, ears trained, like some elongated pixie.

'What are you doing?' Anton asked, as he walked past.

'Watching room seven,' Louise said, and smiled and looked down.

'Are you okay?' Anton said, referring to their conversation in the kitchen that morning.

'I don't know.'

'I know you don't and that's okay.'

'Can you help me down?' Louise asked cheekily, and watched as he glanced at the footstool. 'Whoops!' She kicked away the footstool and Anton smiled and helped her down. The brief contact, the feel of his hands on her waist stirred her senses and made her long to break her self-imposed isolation. She just didn't know how.

'I know we need to talk,' Louise said. 'I just don't know when.'

'That's fine.'

A patient buzzed and he let her go.

'Hello, Carmel,' Louise said, and then saw that Carmel wasn't in bed but in the bathroom, and the noise she was making had Louise instantly push the bell before even going to investigate.

'There's something there,' Carmel said. She was deep-squatting and Emily pulled on gloves with her heart in her mouth. Carmel's baby was breech, and if it was a cord prolapse then it was dire indeed.

Louise pressed the bell in the bathroom in three short bursts as she knelt.

Thankfully it wasn't the cord. Instead two little legs were hanging out. 'Call Stephanie,' Louise said, as Brenda popped her head in the door.

'She's delivering someone,' Brenda said. 'I'll get Anton and the cart.'

'You,' Louise said to Carmel, 'are doing amazingly.' The baby was dangling and it was the hardest thing not to interfere. Instinct meant you wanted traction, to get the head out, but Louise breathed through it, her hands hovering to catch the baby.

She heard or rather sensed that it was Anton who had come in and she went to move aside but he just knelt behind Louise. 'Well done, Carmel,' Anton said.

Louise felt his hand on her shoulder as patiently they waited for Mother Nature to take her course.

It was just so lovely and quiet. Brenda came in

with the cart and stood back. There was a baby about to be born and everyone just let it happen.

Patience was a necessary virtue here.

'That's it,' Louise said. 'Put your hands down and feel your baby,' she said, as the baby simply dropped, and Carmel let out a moan as her baby was delivered into her own and Louise's hands.

'Well done,' Anton said, as Brenda went and got a hot blanket and wrapped it around the mother and infant.

Stephanie arrived then, smiling delightedly.

'Well done, Carmel!'

It had been so nice, so lovely and so much less scary with Anton there—a lovely soft birth. Louise's eyes were glittering with happy tears as finally Carmel was back in bed with her husband beside her and her baby in her arms.

It was lovely to see them all cosy and happy.

'It looks like you might get that Christmas at home after all.' Louise smiled.

'Oh, I'm going home tomorrow,' Carmel said. 'Nothing's going to stop us having the Christmas we want now.'

Later, in the kitchen, pulling a teabag from her

scrubs to make Carmel her only fantastic cup of hospital tea, she saw the hotel card that she had brought in to give Emily.

Was it a ridiculous idea to ask him to be there tomorrow? Did she really have to put him through some strange test?

Yet a part of Louise wanted him to see the other side of her also.

She walked out and saw Anton sitting at the desk, writing up his notes.

'Are you working tomorrow?' Louise asked.

'I am.'

She put the card down.

'It's my photo shoot tomorrow from ten till seven—see if you can get away for an hour or so. I'll leave your name at Reception.'

Anton read the address and then looked up but Louise was gone.

CHAPTER FIFTEEN

IT REALLY WAS the best job in the world.

Well, apart from midwifery, which Louise absolutely loved, but this was the absolutely cherry on the cake, Louise thought as she looked in the mirror.

Her hair was all backcombed and coiffed, her eyes were heavy with black eyeliner and she had lashings of red lipstick on.

All her body was buffed and oiled and then she'd had to suffer the hardship of putting on the most beautiful underwear in the world.

It was such a dark red that it was almost black and it emphasised the paleness of her skin.

And she got to keep it!

Louise smiled at herself in the mirror.

'Okay, they're ready for you, Louise.'

Now the hard work started.

She stepped into the presidential suite and took

off her robe and there was Jeremy in bed, looking all sexy and rumpled but very bored with it all, and there, in the lounge, was Anton.

Oh! She had thought he might manage an hour, she hadn't been expecting him to be here at the start.

He gave her a smile of encouragement and Louise let out a breath and smiled back.

'On the bed, Louise,' Roxy, the director said.

'Morning, Jeremy.' Louise smiled. She had worked with him many times.

'Good morning, Louise.'

It was fun, though it was actually very hard work. There were loads of costume changes and not just for Louise—Jeremy kept having to have his shirt changed as Louise's lipstick wiped off. Cold cream too was Jeremy's friend as her lips left their mark on his stomach.

And not once did Anton frown or make her feel awkward.

As evening fell, the drapes were opened to show London at its dark best, though the Christmas lights would be edited out. This was for Valentine's Day after all.

'He's just home from work,' Roxy said. 'Flowers in hand but there's no time to even give them…'

'Okay.'

Jeremy lifted her up and she wrapped her legs around his hips and crossed her ankles as Roxy gave Jeremy a huge bouquet of dark red roses to hold.

'A bit lower, Louise.'

Louise obliged and as she wiggled her hips to get comfortable on Jeremy's crotch she made everyone, including Anton, laugh as she alluded to his complete lack of response. 'You are so-o-o gay, Jeremy!'

Anton had stayed the whole day. Louise could not believe he'd swapped shifts for her and, better still, clearly Emily's baby was behaving.

At the end of the shoot she put on her robe, feeling dizzy and elated, clutching a huge bag of goodies and ready to head to a smaller room to get changed. Anton joined her and they shared a kiss in the corridor.

'Do you want me to hang up my G-string?' Louise asked, between hot, wet kisses.

'God, no,' Anton said.

'You really don't mind?'

'Mind?' Anton said, not caring what he did to her lipstick.

They were deep, deep kissing and she loved the feel of his erection pressing into her, and then she pulled back and smiled—they must look like two drunken clowns.

'I've booked a room,' Anton said.

'Thank God!'

They made it just past the door. Her robe dropped, her back to the wall, Louise tore at his top because she wanted his skin. Louise worked his zipper and freed him, still frantically kissing as she kicked her panties off. Anton's impatient hands dealt swiftly with a condom and then he lifted her. Louise wrapped her legs around him and crossed her ankles far more naturally this time. She was on the edge of coming as she lowered herself onto him but he slowed things right down as he thrust into her because what he had to say was important.

'I am crazy for you, Louise, and I don't want to change a single thing.'

'I know,' Louise said, 'and I'm crazy about you too.'

She couldn't say more than that because her mouth gave up on words and gave in to the throb between her legs. The wall took her weight then as Anton bucked into her, a delicious come ensuing for them both. Then afterwards, instead of letting her down, he walked her to the bed and let her down there.

'We're going to sort this out, Louise.'

'I know we will.' Louise nodded, except she didn't want to ruin their day with tales of yesterday and it was Christmas tomorrow and Louise didn't want to ruin that again, so instead she smiled.

'I need carbs.'

They shared a huge bowl of pasta, courtesy of room service, and then Louise, who had been up since dawn, fell asleep in his arms. Better than anything, though, was the man who, when anyone else would have been snoring, lay restless beside her and finally kissed her shoulder.

'I'm going to pop into the hospital,' Anton said. 'I've got two women—'

'Go,' Louise said, knowing how difficult it must have been to swap his shift today. 'Call me if something happens with Emily.'

'You don't mind me going in?'

She'd have minded more if he hadn't.

CHAPTER SIXTEEN

TWO PATIENTS WERE on his mind this Christmas Eve and Anton walked into the ward and chatted with Evie.

'Hazel's asleep,' Evie said, as he went through the charts. 'I'd expect you to be called in any time soon, though.'

'How about Emily?'

'Hugh's in with her, he's on call tonight. Stephanie looked in on her an hour ago and there's been no change.'

'Thanks.'

He let Hazel sleep. Anton knew now he would be called if anything happened but, for more social reasons, he tapped on the open door of the royal suite.

'Hi, Anton,' Hugh said. 'All's quiet here.'

'That's good.'

'How was your day off?' Emily asked.

'Good.'

'I was just going to check on a patient.' Hugh stood and yawned.

'I could say the same,' Anton said, 'but I wanted to check in on Emily too.'

'Is this a friendly visit, Anton?' Emily asked when Hugh had left.

'A bit of both,' Anton said, and sat on the bed. 'How are you?'

'I don't know,' Emily admitted. 'I think I've given up hoping for thirty-three weeks.'

'Thirty-one weeks is considered a moderately premature baby,' Anton said. 'Yours is a nice size. I would guess over three pounds in weight and it's had the steroids.'

'How long would it be in NICU?'

'Depends,' Anton said. 'Five weeks, maybe four if all goes well.' He knew this baby was coming and so Anton prepared Emily as best he could. 'All going well with a thirty-one-weeker means there will be some bumps—jaundice, a few apnoea attacks, runs of bradycardia. All these we expect as your baby learns to regulate its temperature and to feed…' He went through it all with her, and even though Emily had been over and over it herself he still clarified some things.

Not once had she cried, Anton thought.

Not since he had done the scan after her appendectomy had he seen Emily shed a tear.

'You can ask me anything,' Anton offered, because she was so practical he just wanted to be sure there was nothing on her mind that he hadn't covered.

'Anything?' Emily said.

'Of course.'

'How was the photo shoot?'

Anton smiled. 'I walked into that one, didn't I?'

'You did.'

'Louise was amazing.'

'She is.'

'Yet,' Anton ventured, 'for someone who is so open about everything, and I mean *everything*, she's very private too…'

'Yes.'

'I'm not asking you to tell me anything,' Anton said.

'You just want her to?'

Anton nodded and then said, 'I want her to feel able to.'

CHAPTER SEVENTEEN

LOUISE OPENED HER eyes to a dark hotel room on Christmas morning and glanced at the time. It was four a.m. and no Anton.

She lay there remembering this time last year but even though she was alone it didn't feel like it this time, especially when the door opened gently and Anton came in quietly.

'Happy Christmas,' Louise said.

'Buon Natale,' Anton said, as he undressed.

'How's Emily?'

'Any time now,' Anton said. 'I was just about to come back here when another patient went into labour.'

'Hazel?' Louise sleepily checked.

'A little girl,' Anton said. 'She's in NICU but I'm very pleased with how she is doing.'

'A nice way to start Christmas,' Louise said, as he slid into bed and spooned into her.

His hands were cold and so was his face as he dropped a kiss on her shoulder.

'Scratch my back with your jaw.'

He obliged and then, without asking, scratched the back of her neck too, his tongue wet and probing, his jaw all lovely and stubbly, and his hand stroking her very close to boiling.

'Did you stop for condoms?'

'No,' Anton said. 'We have one left.'

'Use it wisely, then.' Louise smiled, though she didn't want his hand to move for a second and as Anton sheathed himself Louise made the beginning of a choice—she would have to go on the Pill. They were both so into each other that common sense was elusive, but she stopped thinking then as she felt him nudging her entrance. Swollen from last night and then swollen again with want, it was Louise who let out a long moan as he took her slowly from behind. His hand was stroking her breast and she craned her neck for his mouth.

He could almost taste her near orgasm on her tongue as it hungrily slathered his. He was being cruel, the best type of cruelty because she was going to come now and he'd keep going through it. She almost shot out of her skin as it hit, and she wished he would stop but she also wished he wouldn't. It was so deliciously relentless, there was no come down. Anton started thrusting faster, driving her to the next, and then he stilled and she wondered why because they were just about there…

'No way,' Louise said, hearing his phone. 'Quickly…'

Oh, he tried, but it would not stop ringing. 'Sorry…' Anton laughed at her urgency, because sadly it was his special phone that was ringing. The one for his special Anton patients. And a very naked Louise lay there as he took the call.

'Get used to it,' Anton said as he was connected, and then he hesitated, because if he was telling Louise to get used to it, well, it was something he'd never said before. There was no time to dwell on it, though, as he listened to Evie.

'I'll be there in about fifteen minutes. Thank you for letting me know.' He ended the call.

'Are you coming in with me to deliver a Christmas baby?'

'Emily!'

'Waters just fully broke...'

'Oh, my goodness...'

'She's doing well. Hugh's on his way in but things are going to move quite fast.'

They had the quickest shower ever and then Anton drove them through London streets on a wet, pre-dawn Christmas morning and he got another phone call from the ward. He asked for them to page the anaesthetist for an epidural as that could sometimes slow things down and also, despite the pethidine she'd been given, Emily was in a lot of pain.

'She'll be okay,' Louise said, only more for herself. 'I'm so scared, Anton,' Louise admitted. 'I really am.'

'I know, but she's going to be fine and so is the baby.' There was no question for Anton, they *had* to be okay. 'Big breath,' Anton said.

'I'm not the one in labour.'

It had just felt like it for a moment, though.

Oh, she was terrified for her friend but Louise was at her sparkly best as she and Anton walked into the delivery ward.

'Oh!' Emily smiled in delighted surprise because it was only five a.m. after all.

'The mobile obstetric squad has arrived,' Louise teased. 'Aren't you lucky that it's us two on?' She smiled and gave Emily a cuddle. 'Oh, hi, Hugh!' Louise winked and noted he was looking a bit white. 'Merry Christmas!'

'Hi, Louise.' Hugh was relieved to see them both too.

'I want an epidural,' Emily said.

'It's on its way. I've already paged Rory. We want to slow this down a little,' Anton explained while examining her, 'and an epidural might help us to do that. You've got a bit of a way to go but because the baby is small you don't have to be fully dilated.'

'I'm scared,' Emily admitted.

'You're going to meet your baby,' Louise said, and she gave Emily's hand a squeeze. 'Let us worry for you, okay? We're getting paid after all.'

Emily nodded.

'NICU's been notified?' Anton checked, and then gave an apologetic smile when Evie rolled her eyes and nodded, and Anton answered for her. 'Of course they have.'

There was a knock on the door and Emily's soon-to-be-favourite person came in.

'Hi, lovely Emily,' Rory said. 'We meet again.'

'Oh, yes,' Louise recalled. 'Rory knocked you out when you had your appendix.'

'Hopefully this will slow things down enough that I miss Christmas dinner,' Louise joked, though they all knew this baby would be born by dawn.

A little high on pethidine, a little ready to fix the world, very determined not to panic about the baby, Emily decided she had the perfect solution, the perfect one to show Louise how wonderful and not controlling or jealous Anton was.

And the man delivering your premature baby had to be seriously wonderful, Emily decided!

'Tell them about your Christmas dinner last year,' Emily said, as Louise sat her up and put her legs over the edge of the bed and then pulled Emily in for an epidural cuddle.

'Relax,' Hugh said, stroking Emily's hair as she leant on Louise, while Rory located the position on Emily's spine.

But Emily didn't want to relax, she wanted this sorted now!

'Tell them!' Emily shouted, and Louise shared a little 'yikes' look with Hugh.

Never argue with a woman in transition!

'I'm going to have a word with you later,' Louise warned. She knew what Emily was doing.

'Okay!' Louise said, as she cuddled Emily. 'Well, I'd broken up with Wesley and I checked myself into a hotel—the most miserable place on God's earth, as it turned out, and I couldn't face the restaurant and families so I had room service and it was awful. I think it was processed chicken...'

'Stay still, Emily,' Rory said.

'She's having a contraction,' Anton said, and Louise rocked her through it and after Rory got back to work she went on with her story.

'Well, I was so miserable but I cheered myself up by realising I'd finally got out of having Christmas dinner at Mum's.'

'It's seriously awful food,' Rory said casually, threading the cannula in.

'You wouldn't know,' Louise retorted. 'The one time you came for dinner you pretended you'd been paged and had to leave. Anyway, I arrived at Mum's on Boxing Day and she'd *saved* me not one but about five dinners, and had decided I needed a mother's love and cooking...'

Anton laughed. 'That bad?'

'So, so bad,' Louise said, and her little tale had got them through the insertion of the epidural and she'd managed not to reveal all.

She looked at Anton and there wasn't a flicker of a ruffled feather at her mention of Rory once being at her family's home.

He was a good man. She'd always known it, now she felt it.

'You'll start to feel it working in a few minutes, Emily,' Rory said.

'I can feel it working already.' Emily sighed

in relief as Louise helped her back onto the delivery bed.

Rory left and Louise told Evie she'd got this and then suggested that Anton grab a coffee as she set about darkening the room.

'Sure,' Anton said, even though he didn't feel like leaving, but, confident that he would be called when needed and not wanting to make this birth too different for Emily, he left.

The epidural brought Emily half an hour of rest and she lay on her side, with Hugh beside her as Louise sat on the couch out of view, a quiet presence as they waited for nature to take its course, but thirty minutes later Louise called Anton in.

The room was still quiet and dark but it was a rather full one—Rory and the paediatric team were present for the baby as the baby began its final descent into the world.

'Do you feel like you need to push?' Anton asked, and Emily shook her head as her baby inched its way down.

'A bit,' she said a moment later.

'Try not to,' Anton said. 'Let's do this as slowly as we can.'

'Head end, Hugh,' Louise said, because he looked a bit green, and she left him at Emily's head and went down to the action end, holding Emily's leg as Anton did his best to slow things down.

'Do you want a mirror?' Louise asked.

'Absolutely not.'

'Black hair and lots of it.' Louise was on delighted tiptoe.

'Louise, can you come up here?' Emily gasped. 'I don't want you seeing me…'

'Oh, stop it.' Louise laughed and then Emily truly didn't care what anyone could see because, even with the epidural, there was the odd sensation of her baby moving down.

'Oh!'

'Don't push,' Anton said.

'I think I have to.'

'Breathe,' Hugh said, and got the F word back, but she did manage to breathe through it as Anton helped this little one get a less rapid entrance into the world. And then out came the head and Louise gently suctioned its tiny mouth as its eyes blinked at the new world.

'Happy Christmas,' Anton said, delivering a very vigorous bundle onto Emily's stomach.

Emily got her hotbox blanket wrapped around her shoulders and then another one was placed over a tiny baby whose mum and dad were starting to get to know it.

Anton glanced over at the paediatrician and all was well enough to allow just a minute for a nice cuddle.

'A girl,' Emily said.

The sweetest, sweetest girl, Louise thought. She stood watching over them, holding oxygen near her little mouth as Emily and Hugh got to cuddle her and Louise cried happy tears, baby-just-been-born tears, but then she did what she had to.

'We need to check her...'

And finally Emily started to cry.

CHAPTER EIGHTEEN

LOUISE TOOK THE baby over to the warmer and she was wrapped and given some oxygen and a tube put down her to give her surfactant that would help with her immature lungs.

'We're going to take her up,' Louise said, as Emily completely broke down.

'Can't I go with her?'

'Not yet,' Anton said, 'but you'll be able to see her soon.'

'I'll go with her,' Hugh assured his wife, but Louise could see how upset Emily was. She had been holding onto her emotions for weeks now, quietly determined not to love her baby too much, though, of course she did.

'Hugh, you stay with Emily and I'll stay with the baby,' Louise suggested. 'She's fine, she's beautiful and you'll see her very soon, Emily. I promise I am not going to leave her side.'

Louise did stay with her, the neonatal staff did their thing and Louise watched, but from a chair, smiling when an hour or so later Hugh came in.

'Hi, Dad,' Louise said, watching as Hugh peered in. 'How's Emily?'

'Upset,' Hugh said. 'She'll be fine once she sees her but Anton says she needs to have a sleep first and she won't.' He took out his phone and went to film the baby, who was crying and unsettled.

'Why don't you go and get some colostrum from her?' Ellie, the neonatal nurse, suggested to Louise. 'Mum might feel better knowing she's fed her.'

'Great idea.' Louise smiled and headed back to the ward.

Emily was back in her room, the door open so she could be watched, but the curtains were drawn.

'Knock-knock,' Louise said, and there was her friend, teary and missing her baby so much. 'She's fine, Hugh's with her,' Louise went on, and explained her plans.

'You just need to get a tiny bit off,' Louise said, 'but she's hungry and it's so good to get the colostrum into them.'

'Okay.'

Emily managed a few drops, which Louise nursed into a syringe, but Louise reassured her that that was more than enough. 'This is like gold for your baby.' Louise was delighted with her catch.

As Louise headed out she glanced at the time and realised she would have to ring her mum, who was going to be incredibly worried, given what had happened last year.

As Anton walked into the kitchen on the maternity unit it was to the sight of Louise brightly smiley and taking a selfie with her phone.

'Forward it onto me,' Anton said.

Louise smiled. He didn't care a bit that she was vain, though in this instance he was mistaken. 'Actually, this is for Mum. She's all stressed and thinks I've made up Emily's baby. Well, she didn't say that exactly...' She texted her mum the photo and then picked up the small syringe of colostrum. 'Christmas dinner for Baby Linton. I can't believe she's here.'

'Relieved?' Anton asked.

'So, so relieved. I know she's going to get jaundice and give them a few scares but she is just so lovely and such a nice size…'

'Louise.' Anton caught her arm as she went to go. 'How come you didn't go home last Christmas?'

'I told you, I was pretty miserable.'

'Your family are close.'

'Of course.' She shrugged. 'I just didn't want to upset them…'

'You couldn't put on an act for one day?'

'No…' Her voice trailed off. She hadn't wanted to upset her family on Christmas Day and neither did she want to upset him now. Yet her family had been so hurt by her shutting them out. Louise looked into his eyes and knew that her silence was hurting him too. Everyone in the delivery room except Anton knew what had happened last year and if they were going to have a future, and she was starting to think they might, then it was only fair to tell him.

'I couldn't cover up the bruises. I waited till Boxing Day and called Emily, who came straight away. When I wouldn't go to hospital she called Rory and he came to the hotel and sutured my scalp.'

Louise didn't want to see his expression and neither did she want to go into further details of the day right now. She had told him now and she could feel his struggle to react, to suppress, possibly just to breathe as he fathomed just what the saying meant about having the living daylights knocked out of you. The light in Louise had gone out that day and had stayed out for some months, but it was fully back now. 'I'm going to get this up to the baby.' She kissed his taut cheek. 'You need to shave.'

They had a small, fierce cuddle that said more than words could and then Louise said she was heading up to NICU, still unable to meet his eyes.

Hugh watched and Louise did the filming as

Baby Linton was given the precious colostrum and a short while later was asleep.

Have a sleep now, Louise texted. Your daughter is and she attached the film and sent it.

A few moments later Hugh's phone buzzed and he smiled as Emily gave him the go-ahead.

'Thanks,' Hugh said, and then he took out a pen and crossed out the 'Baby' on 'Baby Linton'. He wrote the word 'Louise' in instead.

Louise Linton.

'Two Ls means double the love,' Louise said, trying not to cry. 'Thanks, Hugh, that means an awful lot.'

More than anyone could really know.

When Hugh went back to Maternity to be with Emily, Louise sat there, staring at her namesake, and the thought she had briefly visited that morning returned.

She'd have to go back on the Pill. It wouldn't be fair to Anton if there were any mistakes, however unlikely it was that she might naturally fall pregnant. But that ultimately meant, when she came off the Pill again, another few months of the horrible times she'd just been through simply trying to work out her cycle.

Louise knew she was probably looking at another year at best. Could she do it without sulking? Louise wondered. Just let go of her hopes for a baby and chase the dream of a relationship that actually worked?

She walked over and looked at the little one who had caused so much angst but who had already brought so many smiles.

'How's Louise?' Anton came up a couple of hours later and saw Louise standing and gazing into the incubator.

'Tired,' Louise said, still not able to meet his eyes after her revelation. 'Oh, you mean the baby? She's perfect.' She glanced over to where Rory and several staff were gathered around an incubator. Louise knew that it was Henry, a baby she had delivered in November. He had multiple issues and was a very sick baby indeed. She looked down at little Louise, who was behaving beautifully. 'You're a bit of a fraud really, aren't you?'

'Emily's asleep,' Anton said. 'When she wakes up she can come and visit.'

'I'll stay till then.' Louise smiled. 'Can you just watch Louise while I go to the loo?'

Anton glanced over at the neonatal nurse but that wasn't what Louise meant. 'No, you're to be on love watch,' Louise said.

Anton took a seat when usually he wouldn't have and looked at the very special little girl.

'Thank you!' Louise was back a couple of minutes later. 'I really needed that!'

Anton rolled his eyes as Louise, as usual, gave far too much information. When Anton didn't get up she perched on his knee, with her back to him, watching little Louise asleep. She had nasal cannulas in but she was breathing on her own and though she might need a little help with that in the coming days, for now she was doing very well.

'Emily's here,' Anton said, and Louise jumped up and smiled as Emily was wheeled over.

Yes, Louise was far from the tiniest infant here

but the machines and equipment were terrifying and Ellie talked them through it.

'I'm going to go,' Louise said, and gave Emily a kiss. 'I'll come and see you tomorrow. Send me a text tonight. Oh, and here...' She handed over a little pink package. 'Open it later. Just enjoy your time with her now.'

She gave her friend a quick cuddle then she and Anton left them to it.

'Do you want to come to Mum and Dad's?' Louise asked, as they stopped by his office to get his laptop.

'Will it cause a lot of questions for you?'

'Torrents,' Louise said, but then the most delicious smell diverted her and she peeked out the door, to see Alex and Jennifer heading onto the ward with two plates and lots of containers.

'Alex,' Louise called, and they turned round.

'They're up seeing the baby,' Louise explained.

'Oh, we didn't come to see them,' Jennifer said, and Louise jumped in.

'How sweet of you to bring Christmas dinner for the obstetrician and midwife,' Louise teased, watching Jennifer turn purple as Anton stepped out.

'Anton.' Alex smiled warmly. 'Merry Christmas.'

'Merry Christmas,' Anton said.

'You haven't met Jennifer...'

'Jennifer.' Anton smiled. 'Merry Christmas.'

'Merry Christmas,' Jennifer croaked, and then turned frantic eyes to Louise. 'We don't want to disturb Emily and Hugh, we were just going to leave them a dinner for tonight...' She was practically thrusting the plates at Louise. 'We'll leave these with you.'

But Louise refused to be rushed.

'That's so nice of you,' Louise said, but instead of taking the plates she peeked under the foil. 'Jennifer, Emily didn't just give birth to a foal—there's enough here to feed a horse.'

It looked and smelt amazing and Louise was shameless in her want for a taste, not just for her but for Anton too. 'That's what a traditional Christmas dinner looks like, Anton.' Louise smiled sweetly at Jennifer. 'It's Anton's first

Christmas in England,' Louise explained, and of course she would get her way. 'What a shame he's never tasted a really nice one.'

'I'm sure there's enough for everyone,' Alex said, oblivious to his wife's tension around Anton, and Jennifer gave in.

'Luckily my husband's good with a scalpel!'

It was a very delicate operation.

They went into the kitchen and got out tea plates.

Louise and Anton got two Brussels sprouts each, one roast potato and two slivers of parsnips in butter as Anton watched, fascinated by the argument taking place.

'I don't think Emily needs six piggies in blankets,' Louise said.

'Piggies in blankets?' Anton checked.

'Sausages wrapped in bacon,' Alex translated.

'Two each, then,' Jennifer said, and Alex added them to the tea plates.

'How much turkey can they have?' Alex asked.

'A slice each,' Jennifer said. 'Emily needs her protein.'

Louise shook her head.

'Okay, one and a half,' Jennifer relented.

Alex duly divided.

They got one Yorkshire pudding each too, as well as home-made cranberry and bread sauce, and finally dinner was served!

'You can go now.' Louise smiled. 'Merry Christmas.'

She put sticky notes on Hugh and Emily's plates, warning everyone to keep their greedy mitts off, then Louise closed the kitchen door.

She found a used birthday candle among the ward's Christmas paraphernalia and stuck it in a stale mince pie as their Christmas dinners rotated in the microwave and then she turned the lights off.

'Do you want to pull a cracker?'

'Bon-bon,' Anton said, but they cracked two and sat in hats and, oh, my, Jennifer's cooking was divine, even if you had to fight her to taste it.

'How do you know Jennifer?' Louise asked, as she smeared bread sauce over her turkey.

'I don't.'

'Anton!' Louise looked at his deadpan face. 'No way was that the first time you two have met. Is she pregnant again?' Louise frowned. 'She must be in her mid-forties…'

'I don't know what you're on about,' Anton said, though his lips were twitching to tell.

'Are you having an affair with Jennifer?' Louise asked, smiling widely.

'Where the hell did you produce that from?' Anton smiled back.

'Anton, Jennifer went purple when she saw you and I just know you've seen each other before.'

'I don't know if I like this bread sauce,' was Anton's response to her probing.

'It's addictive,' Louise said, and gave up fishing.

It was the nicest Christmas dinner ever—perfect food, the best company and a baby named Louise snug and safe nearby. After they had finished their delectable meal Louise went over and sat on his knee. 'Thank you for a lovely Christmas, Anton.'

'Thank you,' Anton said, because what she'd told him, though upsetting, hadn't spoiled his Christmas. Instead, it had drawn them closer.

'We both deserve it, I think.'

She felt his arms on her back, lightly stroking the clasp of her bra and as she rested her head on his shoulder it felt the safest place in the world.

'Do you understand why I'm so wary?'

'Now I do,' Anton said. 'I'm glad you were able to tell me and I am so sorry for what happened to you.'

It was then Louise let her dreams go; well, not for ever, but she put them on hold for a while.

'I'm going to cancel my appointment,' Louise said, and she didn't lift her head, not now because she couldn't look him in the eye but because she didn't want Anton to see her cry. 'Well, I'm going to go and get the test results back but I'm not going to go for the IVF.'

He could hear her thick voice and knew there were tears and he rubbed her back.

'Thank you,' Anton said, and they sat for a moment, Anton glad for the chance for them, Louise grateful for it too but just a bit sad for now, though she soon chirped up.

'When I say cancelling the IVF I meant that I'm postponing it,' Louise amended. 'No pressure or anything but I'm not waiting till I'm forty for you to make up your mind whether you want us to be together.'

'You have to make your mind up too,' Anton pointed out.

'Oh, I did yesterday,' Louise said, and pulled her head back and smiled into his eyes. 'I'm already in.' She gave him a light kiss before standing to head for home.

'You're stuck with me now.'

CHAPTER NINETEEN

As they walked out they bumped into Rory, who was on his way up to NICU to check in on a six-week-old who was doing his level best to spoil everyone's Christmas.

'You look tired,' Louise said.

'Very,' Rory admitted. 'I'm just off to break some bad news to a family.'

'What time do you finish?' Louise asked.

'Six.'

'Do you want to come for a rubbish dinner at Mum's?' Louise asked.

'God, no.' Rory smiled.

'Honestly, if Anton and you *both* come then Mum will assume I'm just bringing all the strays and foreigners who are lonely…' she pointed her thumb in Anton's direction '…rather than grilling me about him.' She knew Rory's family lived miles away. 'You don't want to be on your own on Christmas night.'

'I won't be on my own,' Rory said. 'Thanks for offering, though. I'm going to Gina's to help her celebrate her first sober Christmas in who knows how long.'

'Gina?' Louise checked. 'Is she the one you're—?'

'She's always been the one,' Rory said. 'It's nearly killed me to watch her self-destruct.' He stood there on the edge of breaking down as Anton's hand came on his shoulder. 'Nothing's ever happened between us,' Rory explained. 'And nothing can.'

'Why?' Louise asked.

'Because she's in treatment and you're not supposed to have a relationship for at least a year.'

'Does she know how you feel?' Louise asked.

'No, because I don't want to confuse her. She's trying to sort her stuff out and I don't want to add to it.'

'She's so lucky to have you,' Louise said, 'even if she doesn't know that she has.' Louise let out a breath. 'Who's going to speak to the parents with you?'

'Just me,' Rory said. 'They're all busy with Henry.'

'I know the parents,' Louise said to Rory. 'You're not doing that on your own. Is there any hope?'

'A smudge,' Rory said, and they headed back to NICU and Anton stood and waited as Louise and Rory went in to see the parents.

Anton loved her love.

How she gave it away and then, when surely there should be nothing left, she still gave more.

How she walked so pale out of a horrible room and cuddled her ex as Anton stood there, the least jealous guy in the world. He was simply glad that Rory had Louise to lean on as Anton remembered that horrible Christmas when he'd been the one breaking bad news.

He would be grateful to Rory for ever for being there for Louise last year.

As they walked out into the grey Christmas afternoon and to Anton's car, Louise spoke.

'Rory's right not to tell Gina how he feels,' Louise said.

'Do you think?'

'I do.' Louise nodded. 'I think you do need a whole year to recover from anything big. Not close to a year, you need every single day of it, you need to go through each milestone, each anniversary and do them differently, and as of today I have.'

It had been a hard year, though the previous one had been harder—estranged from family and friends and losing herself in the process. But now here she was, a little bit older, a whole lot wiser, and certainly Louise was herself.

Yes, she was grateful for those difficult years.

It had brought her here after all.

CHAPTER TWENTY

'Ooh…' Louise reached for her phone as it bleeped. 'We do need to stop on our way to the hotel for condoms because it would seem that I just ovulated.'

'You get an alert when you ovulate?' Anton shook his head in disbelief.

'Well, I put in all my cycles and temperatures and things and it calculates it. It's great…'

'You're going to be one of those old ladies who talks about her bowels, aren't you?'

'God, yes.' Louise laughed at the thought. 'I'll probably have an app for it.'

The thing was, Anton wanted to be the old man to see it.

'Where's a bloody chemist when you need one?' Louise grumbled, going through her phone as Anton drove on and came to the biggest, yet ultimately the easiest decision of his life.

'We could stop at a pub,' Louise suggested. 'Nip in to the loos and raid the machines.'

'We're not stopping, Louise. You need to get to your mum's.'

Louise sulked all the way back to the hotel and even more so when they came out of the elevator and she swiped her entry card to their room. 'I've got the hotel room, a hot Italian and no bloody condoms. Where's the justice, I ask you…'

And then the door opened and she simply stopped speaking. For a moment Louise thought she had the wrong room because it was in darkness save for the twinkling fairly-lights reflecting off the tinsel. She had never seen a room more overly decorated, Louise thought. There was green, silver, red and gold tinsel, there were lights hanging everywhere. It was gaudy, it was loud and so, so beautiful.

'You did this?'

'I don't want you ever to think of a hotel room on Christmas Day and be sad again. I want this to be your memory.'

'How?'

'I rang them,' Anton said. 'They were worried it looked over the top, but I reassured them you can *never* have too much tinsel.'

'It's the nicest thing you could have done.'

'Yet,' Anton said, for he intended many nice things for Louise.

They started to kiss, a lovely long kiss that led them to bed. A kiss that had them peeling off their clothes and Louise stared up at the twinkling lights as slowly he removed her underwear, kissing her everywhere.

'Anton...' She was all hot and could barely breathe as he removed her bra and kissed her breasts. Louise unwrapped her presents with haste; Anton took his time.

'Anton...' she pleaded, touching herself in frustration as he slid down her panties, desperate for the soft warmth of his mouth.

'Your turn next,' Louise said, as, panties off, he kissed up her thigh. Right now she just wanted to concentrate on the lovely feel of his mouth there, except his mouth now teased her stomach and then went back to her breasts, swirling them with his tongue and then working back up to her mouth.

His erection was there, nudging her entrance, teasing her with small thrusts, and her hands balled in frustration.

'We don't have any—'

'Do you want to try for a baby?' Anton said, throwing caution to a delectable wind that had chased him for, oh, quite a while now.

'Our baby?' Louise checked.

'I would hope so.' Anton smiled.

'You're sure?'

'Very,' Anton said. 'But are you?'

He didn't need to ask twice, but the ever-changing Louise changed again, right there in his arms.

'I'm very sure, but it isn't just a baby I want now. I want to have a baby with you,' Louise said.

'You shall,' Anton said, and it brought tears to her eyes because here was the man she loved, who would do all he could to make sure her dream came true.

The feel of him unsheathed driving into her had Louise let out a sob of pleasure. For Anton, it was heady bliss. Sensations sharpened, and he felt the warm grip and then the kiss of her cervix, welcoming him over and over again, till for Anton that was it.

The final swell of him, the passion that shot into her tipped Louise deep into orgasm. Her legs tight around him, she dragged him in deeper and let out a little scream. Then she held him there for her pleasure, just to feel each and every pulse and twitch from them as his breathing made love to her ear.

She looked up at the twinkling lights and never again would she think of Christmas and not remember this.

'What are you doing?' Anton spoke to the pillow as, still inside her, Louise's hand reached across the bed.

'Taking a photo,' Louise said, aiming her camera at the fairy-lights. And capturing the moment, she knew she'd found love, for ever.

CHAPTER TWENTY-ONE

'WILL IT BE a problem, us working together?' Louise asked. They were back at her home, with Louise grabbing everyone's presents from under her tree. 'Honestly, it's something we need to speak about.'

'We'll be fine,' Anton said. 'Louise, the reason I came down harder on you than anyone is because of what happened in Italy that day when it did all go wrong…but you're an amazing midwife, over and over I've seen it. Aside from personally, I love working with you. I know that the patients get the very best care.'

'Thank you,' Louise said. 'Still, if we get sick of each other…' She stopped then and looked at the amazing man beside her. She could never get tired of looking at him, working alongside him, getting to know him.

'I got you two presents,' Louise said.

He opened the first annoying slowly. It was beautifully wrapped and he took his time then smiled at black and white sweets wrapped in Cellophane.

'Humbugs,' Louise said, and popped one in her mouth and then gave him a very nice kiss.

'Peppermint,' Anton replied, having taken it from her mouth.

He opened the other present a little more quickly, given its strange shape, to find a large pepperoni.

'Reminds me of,' Louise teased, 'my first kiss with the pizza man and I'm also ensuring that if we ever do break up then you will never be able to eat pepperoni, or taste mint, without thinking of me. I've just hexed you orally.'

'You *are* a witch!'

'I am!' Louise smiled.

'Then you would know already that I love you.'

'I do.' Louise's eyes were misty with tears as he confirmed his feelings.

'And, if you are a witch, you would know just

how much I love you and that I would never, ever hurt you.'

'I do know that,' Louise said. 'And if you're my wizard you'll already know that I love you with all my heart.'

'I do.'

'But I'm about to make you suffer.' She smiled at his slight frown. 'We need to get to Mum's.'

Louise's family were as mad as the woman they had produced.

Anton watched as they tore open their presents.

'A cookery book?' Susan blinked. 'Oh, and a lesson. It's a lovely thought, Louise, but I don't need a cookery lesson...'

'It's for charity, Mum.'

'I could teach her a thing or three,' Susan said, 'but I suppose if it's for charity...' She smiled a bright smile. 'Time for dinner. It's so late, you must all be starving.'

They headed to the dining room, which was decorated with so much tinsel that Anton realised where Louise's little problem stemmed from.

At first Anton had no idea what Louise was talking about when she had moaned about her mother's cooking.

It looked as good as Jennifer's, it even smelt as good as Jennifer's, but, oh, my, the taste.

'That,' Anton said, after an incredibly long twenty minutes, putting down his knife and sweating in relief that he'd cleared his plate, 'was amazing, Susan.'

'There's plenty more.' Susan smiled as she collected up the plates.

Anton looked over at Louise's dad, who gave him a thumbs-up.

'Christmas pudding now,' he said. 'Home-made!'

'If you get through this,' Chloe, Louise's younger sister, whispered to him, 'you're in.'

The lights went down and a flaming pudding was brought in and they all duly sang, except for Anton because he didn't know the words.

It looked amazing, dark and rich and smothered in brandy crème, though had he not had a taste of Jennifer's delectable one then Anton would, there and then, have sworn off Christmas pudding for life.

It was a very small price to pay for love, though.

'Family recipe.' Susan winked, as she sat down to eat hers.

'It's wonderful, Mum,' Louise said.

In its own way it was, so much so that Louise decided to share the smile.

'I'm going to take a photo and send it to my friends,' Louise said, as her mother beamed with pride. 'They don't know what they're missing out on!'

Later they crashed on the sofa and watched a film. Anton sat and Louise lay with her head in his lap. Her sisters were going through the Valentine bras she had left over from the shoot. 'There's your namesake,' Louise said, munching on chocolate as Ebenezer Scrooge appeared on screen. Anton smiled. He had never been happier.

He even smiled as Louise's sister wrinkled her nose. 'What's that smell?'

'Mum's making kedgeree for Boxing Day.' Louise yawned.

'What's kedgeree?' Anton asked.

'Rice, eggs, haddock, curry powder.' Louise looked up and met his gaze.

'How about tomorrow we go shopping for a ring?' Anton said.

'Did you just propose?'

'I did.'

'Louise Rossi…' she mused. 'I like it.'

'Good.'

'And I love you.'

'I love you too.'

'But if you're buying my ring in the Boxing Day sales, I expect a really big one, and if we're engaged, then you can tell me what's going on with you and Jennifer.'

'When I get the ring I'll tell you.'

'Mum,' Louise called, 'Dad, we just got engaged.'

There were smiles and congratulations and

after a very dry December Anton enjoyed the champagne as he pulled out his phone. 'I'd better ring my family and tell them the news. They're loud,' he warned.

There were lots of *'complimentes!'* and *'salute!'* on speaker phone as glasses were raised. Much merriment later they came to the rapid decision they would go over there for the New Year and see them and, yes, it would seem they were officially engaged.

Louise checked her own phone and there was a picture of Hugh and Emily sharing a gorgeous Christmas dinner, courtesy of Jennifer and Alex. There was a text too, thanking them for the little pink outfit and hat, which they were sure Baby Louise would be wearing very soon.

There was also a text from Rory and it made her smile.

'How's that smudge of hope?' Anton asked, referring to little Henry.

'Still smudging.' Louise smiled as she read Rory's text. 'It's sparkling apple juice his end and I've been given strict instructions that we're not to say anything, ever, to anyone, about what he said today.'

'I am very glad that Gina has Rory with her,' Anton said.

'And me,' Louise said, and then looked up at the man she would love for ever. 'You do know that you're going to be sleeping on the sofa tonight?'

'Am I?'

'My parents would freak otherwise.' She smiled again. 'Did you know that I'm a twenty-nine-year-old virgin?'

'Of course you are,' Anton said, and stroked her hair. He'd sleep in the garden if he had to.

Louise lay there, her family nearby, Anton's hands in her hair, and all felt right with the world.

Just so completely right.

'I think that I might already be pregnant,' Louise whispered.

'Don't start.' Anton smiled.

'No, I really think I am. I feel different.'

'Stop it.' Anton laughed.

But, then, Anton thought, knowing Louise,

knowing how meant to be they were, she possibly was.

They might just have made their own Christmas baby.

* * * * *